LETTERS FROM THE REALMS OF NERO

GEORGE KAPO

Published by JW Cochrane 2007

Copyright © JW Cochrane 2007

All Rights Reserved. No part of this publication may be reproduced or transmitted in any form or by any means, electronic or mechanical, including photocopier, recording or any other information storage and retrieval system, without prior permission in writing from the publisher of this book.

First published in United Kingdom 2007 by
JW Cochrane, 1 Fielden Place, Bracknell, RG12 2PB

Printed and bound in the United Kingdom by
Think Ink 01473 400162

A CIP catalogue record for this book is available from the British Library.

This book is sold subject to the condition that it shall not, by way of trade or otherwise be lent, resold, hired out, or otherwise circulated without the publisher's prior consent in any form of binding or cover other than that in which it is published and without a similar condition including this condition being imposed on the subsequent purchaser.

ISBN 978 0 9557862 0 4

A Brief Profile of George Kapo

His father, Count George Vsevolod Kapolenko, the son of a minor Russian Imperial Prince, joined General Wrangel's White Russian Army, in southern Russia about 1918. There he fought with the Cossack cavalry against the overwhelming Bolshevik Red Army; finally joining the forced evacuation from the Crimea in 1920.

He united with his family who had fortuitously moved a good part of their wealth and later themselves, to the safety of Switzerland. From there he moved to Paris to study Classics at the Sorbonne. He became a nationalised Frenchman and joined the French Diplomatic Corps.

In 1930 he fell out with his father, he refused to use his titles and shortened his name to Kapo. He had married for love: a marriage not arranged by his family and not approved of by hers. She was from a wealthy Jewish banking family; they asked for nothing from their respective families and received less.

George was born five years later, their third and last child. He was named after his grandfather, in an effort to soften hearts. The Kapo's fled to Britain, ahead of the May 1940 Nazi invasion of France, to the new family home overlooking the River Thames at Caversham. George lives there to this day.

His father died when the American aircraft a Norsman C-65, shuttling him to Paris went missing over France on the 15th December 1944; he was working for General DeGaulle. Also on that flight was the famous American band leader, Major Glen Miller. Icing due to poor weather conditions, was probably the cause of the disappearing single engine nine seater aircraft.

George studied Classics at Oxford; he had learnt his Russian and French from his parents. His mother, a talented amateur musician encouraged her family to play. George practised the double base, but never excelled, unlike his siblings who both pursued musical careers.

His mother hated the notion of him joining the army, and he freely admits that his mother badgered him into taking a post at the BBC Monitoring Station, Caversham; in order to avoid his national service. He started as a translator and was still there in 1990 when he retired.

He will tell you with a wry smile, that his father spent his eventful life opposing tyranny whereas; he has spent a dull lifetime listening to the tedious propaganda of tyrants. He has maintained a passion for the ancient world from his university days and has published a book and a few papers on the subject. George has never married and now lives with his widowed sister.

Contents

Introduction 1

Chapter 1 Letters Concerning 7
A new slave, her new environment Rome, and her duties.

Chapter 2 Letters Concerning 23
Planets talks of Britain and how the Romans saved her tribe.
A meeting with the Emperor and his mistress Acte.

Chapter 3 Letters Concerning 42
Planets' adventures leaving Britain. The murder of the city prefect.
Acte makes a plea for her baby. Cinnamus talks of Paul of Tarsus.

Chapter 4 Letters Concerning 62
Queen Boudicca's rebellion; Ninth Legion disaster.

Chapter 5 Letters Concerning 77
Cinnamus contemplates marriage and consults an astrologer.
A delegation of priests arrive from Jerusalem. Seneca retires from Rome.

Chapter 6 Letters Concerning 89
The wedding. Seneca in peril. The move to Nomentum.

Chapter 7 Letters Concerning 105
Faenius Rufus and others fall to Tiggellinus. Nero divorces Octavia.
How Britannicus and Agrippina died. Nero marries Poppaea.

Chapter 8 Letters Concerning 116
Business in the senate. Poppaea's princess. Cinnamus becomes a father.
The cult of Osiris.

Chapter 9 Letters Concerning..................................... 126
Rome burns. Scribonia's wayward daughter.
Pleasures of the bath. Nero builds a new palace and garden.

Chapter 10 Letters Concerning 148
A revolt of gladiators. Naval catastrophe. Death in the house of Seneca.
Verriculla assumes authorship.

Chapter 11 Letters Concerning...................................162
Acte and Julius move in. Dido's gold, a tail of credulity. Nero performs.
The death of Poppaea. Cinnamus goes to Liguria. Various demises.
Paullina's revelations.

Appendix... 175
How the letters were discovered.

Map of Rome... 6

House plan Rome 18

House plan Nomentum 103

Acknowledgements

Ladies of note, who have come to my rescue un-baffling the complexities of the computer:

Mrs Suzanne Cochrane.
Mrs Fiona Mullaney.

A veritable wizard, of the wonders of Adobe Photoshop:

Alexander Gray.

The pedant extraordinaire, whose unfailing attention to my grammar and typos, not misspellings you understand, has rendered this tome readable is:

Mr Bob Brooks of Bracknell College.

For his infectious enthusiasm and his extensive knowledge and stunning photos' he has brought to his lectures on British archaeology. All the way from the Kellogg College of Continuing Education, Oxford University:

Archaeologist Roger Goodburn.
Ably assisted by researcher
Sally Stow.

Dear reader, please join me in metaphorical applause for the worthies above (pause) and they have en mass responded with a graceful and courteous bow.

Introduction

This little story is part fiction, and as far as can be determined part fact. Where the joins are, are for the reader to determine, if he or she should be so inclined, if not relax in your chair and enjoy the read. Students and those who have knowledge of the years covered in the story will derive, I hope, enjoyment in exercising their opinion as to whether life in that time was really like that, or not. If your knowledge is scanty, I can assure you with all the confidence of a double-glazing salesman, that the whole thing is totally accurate down to the last syllable. To add to your pleasure I have included page notes to save you the trouble of reaching for the reference book, as I know it is inconvenient particularly when ensconced in the smallest room, enthralled by the story but hindered from a quick exit. Please ignore them if you will, they are not necessary for understanding the story, or if perhaps you are a clever clogs and don't need them.

Now, I must warn you that this little story contains very little salacious or violent material. However, it does contain a description of a Roman marriage; Roman marriages were designed to produce babies nine months hence. Sensitive souls may avert their eyes to save their blushes when reading this section.

We live in a violent world, but their world was crueller, it was on display; cruelty was entertainment. Nero was not a lover of cruelty for its own sake and Seneca his tutor, positively disparages it. Nero and Seneca were not typical of their time. Now don't throw the story down in disgust, thinking it will be boring, it does contain a lot of jolly interesting stuff on the Emperor Nero, his mother, wives, mistresses, his old tutor Seneca, and the disagreeable man who supplanted him, causing Seneca's suicide.

The main story contains the history of how a little girl from Sussex, England, found herself a slave in Seneca's household, working there under his chief scribe, and how she returned to England for a period after the ravages of Boudicca. It is a story of her good fortune, and how everything worked out fine for her, against a background of disaster for many of the hapless great families of the Empire.

Now, I should not be telling you all this. I should allow the real George Kapo, to do his own introduction. Although, quite frankly he can be a bit stuffy and old fashioned, his translation is very good and he seems tolerably clued-up. I suppose we must let him have his say.

"In the year 1992, I received via my publisher, a letter posted in Zagreb, written in Russian from Dr. Geza Vermes; my own edited translation follows.

'Dear Sir,

I am unknown to you. However, I have read and admired your works published in Russian and request your help. My uncle discovered codices hidden in a lead box in a cave in Slovenia when fighting with the partisans during the Second World War. His brother, my father, the late Geza Vermes emeritus Professor of Greek and Latin at Belgrade University, recovered them later. Their date of origin is from the First Century a.d. They are letters written in the Glagolitic alphabet. My father translated them into Russian. The letters contain material concerning Nero: his court and tutor Seneca, Britain and the Boudicca revolt, the nascent Christian church and Paul of Tarsus. It would be of considerable interest in Britain, as the intimate lives of the people of Rome and their new province of

Britain, are revealed. I would appreciate your advice on this matter.

Yours Sincerely
Dr G Vermes'

The only book of mine that I have translated and published in the Soviet Union was "Slavery in the Roman Empire". It was written at a time when the subject was dear to Soviet historians and to the Communist party, providing the correct conclusions were drawn; this was the time of Stalin's purges. I was amazed that a copy existed in Zagreb and still being read! Still more amazed that Geza Vermes, on the strength of it, had chosen me to reveal to the English speaking world, his uncle's remarkable discovery. These are the letters from which the story is taken.

Traditionally, the origins of the Glagolitic alphabet are ascribed to the saints Cyril (827-868) and his brother Methodios (826-885) it is a conglomerate of Greek, Hebrew and Samaritan scripts with the possibility that it was also based on ancient pre-Christian Slavic runes, similar to the old Nordic runes. There was much antagonism to the brother Saints using this text, in the conversion of the Slavic tribes to Christianity, but they prevailed and it is still used in Churches along the Adriatic seaboard today. Therefore, these codices (pages rather than Scrolls) would be more than nine hundred years old, if genuine!

Papyrus, the original organic material on which the letters would have been written in scroll form, degrades under normal conditions. Therefore, necessitating repeated copying, eventually being transcribed onto the codices format; this occurred concurrent with the introduction of parchment around the eighth century.

They no doubt owed their survival to their important content matter referring to the early church and may well have been used as evidence in the heated and often violent debates on the nature of god/s. It is also worth considering the inferences of Paul's Epistles to Seneca, and Seneca's to Paul. These letters are not included in the canon of the Bible and also originate at a very early date. Most modern scholars consider them 'not of the hand of either Paul or Seneca but later.' There are only slight references to Paul in our work and we must consider the possibility of additional text, supplemented by zealous monkish copyists.

Eagerly, I made arrangements and headed off to Zagreb at the first opportunity. The story I received from Dr. Geza Vermes of how the codices were discovered, I have included in an appendix at the back of this book. It necessarily has details of his family history during the Second World War, the Balkan recovery under Tito and the decline after his death.

What follows, is my free translation into English, from the translation into Russian by Geza's late father, Professor Vermes. I have edited it to make a continuing narrative of the original series of letters, albeit arranged into headed chapters, my aim being to render a smooth, and I hope enjoyable read of these fascinating documents for the general public. I expect criticism from the classicists, who perform their own translations direct from the original, they debate and cavil over the exegesis within these letters and argue over their veracity; that is, of course how they earn their living.

I have endeavoured to render this work for the interested, but non-expert reader. However, the page notes will assist the reader and provide extra information. The reader may prefer to ignore them and enjoy the society of Rome through the eyes of our letter writers. In many ways their standards and morals are at variance to ours, life was more precarious, the need to procreate more urgent. A marriage to a 13 year old is quite normal and legal. The treatment of slaves had improved in imperial times, compared to the republic of 70 years earlier. Although, in Seneca they had a master of exceptional humanity and Nero himself only killed off his mother, half-brother and first wife out of necessity. His fears and farces are related here. Nero is doomed by his youth, he is aged by his unbridled power, we can see him degenerate as Seneca loses influence and sycophants take over, resulting in Seneca's suicide. It is the detail of the lives of the lower orders that make these letters of exceptional interest, how they earn their living, how they survive and prosper, how some of them died in the great fire and how a young slave girl descended into the world of prostitution.

Subsequent radio-carbon dating of the parchment, its wooden binding, and the carbon ink confirms the ninth to tenth century date of the script. It does not rule out the possibility of forgery. I consider it genuine. Some academics disagree, maintaining that they are a palimpsest, that is, they are over- written on an old parchment having the original ink scraped off.

George Kapo.

Rome at the time of Nero

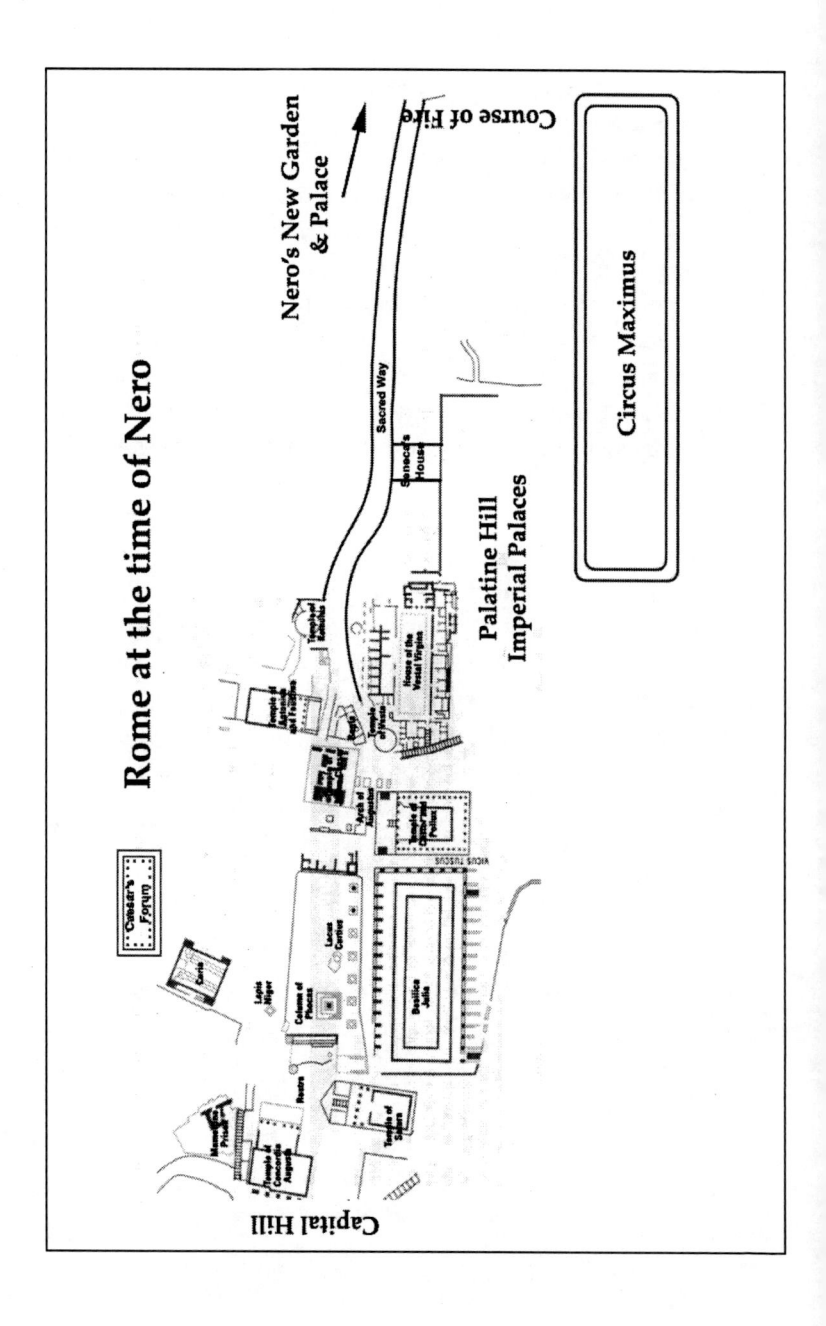

Letters from the Realms of Nero

Chapter 1
A new slave, her new environment Rome, and her duties.

You want to know what Planets told me about our new province of Britain. First, you shall know her true British name and why the cognomen Planets. She came up for auction on a cold, dull and windy day. The last lot of the auction, alone on the dais, a naked, cold, ten-year-old girl, glancing apprehensively around the murmuring crowd while trying to avoid the auctioneers prodding stick as he jabbed it into her flesh to make her turn round.

"This one calls herself Verriculla. But I call her Planets, on account of her eyes," the auctioneer joked. Nobody laughed; they had missed the joke, luckily for me as it turned out. In calling her Planets, he was referring to the fact that one eye wandered in a different direction to the other. The crowd assumed he meant she had a tendency to wander off or run away, therefore, the bidding was light and I struck a bargain for my Master. Thereafter, she always answered to Planets or Lucky Planets in our household and she was never cold again.[1]

Damn fool I reflected, allowing sentiment to overcome common sense, she is probably as tame as a feral cat and speaks less Latin! Having been enslaved myself, I felt the anguish and humiliation of the sale, of never knowing where you will end up and what troubles await you; pity had clouded my better judgment when her glance fell upon me. At least I was from the east and

---

[1] Planet: wandering star: Greek

educated. She was from barbarian Britain, but her left foot was marked to denote a Latin speaker, of course, we all know the tricks of the trade: teach them a few words to pass them off as erudite.

The trader assured me that she would make an excellent servant,

"Being just the right age, with fine teeth, robust health, quick and eager to please," this he said with a knowing wink. After I parted with my denarii and thereby taking ownership; the dealer, her previous owner, proffered in my ear out of the hearing of the auctioneer that, should I be requiring any future purchases he would always consider a private deal, including part exchange at special prices for such an honoured and a discerning customer as I. I wondered if I looked as gullible as I felt.

The rain, which had started to fall at the conclusion of the deal, dampened my clothing, as the deal had dampened my ego. Planets, however, had now attired herself in a hooded woollen cape. With the hood covering her head, she kept her self both dry and warm. I noticed it gave off an ever-increasing odour of rancid sheep grease, as it got progressively damper and warmer. Planets kept her head down looking at the pavement (with one eye at least) stamping her foot and twisting it against the pavement. To try out her Latin and to satisfy my curiosity, I proffered the question,

"What are you doing?" To my surprise, she answered,

"Trying to see where the mud has gone." Her answer, although naïve pleased me greatly, I felt less gullible; she had a limited ability to speak and understand some Latin at least. As we perambulated along the forum pavement,[2] I could not suppress a little smile, and thought to try further conversation. Pausing to look around at the colonnade that surrounded us, I told her authoritatively, that Julius Caesar built this forum and paved it with flag stones to keep the mud at bay; and that he was the first Roman to set foot in Britain.

"Twice," she said.

"Twice?" I asked, surprised.

"Yes, twice, he came to Britain twice when he conquered Gaul. He came to buy grain." Encouraged and even more surprised, I walked her over to Caesar's statue.

"And there he is" I said as we stood before Caesar; she stared at it closely, closing one eye.

"And why did the gods turn him into stone? Is it because he told wicked lies claiming he built all this?" She gesticulated about her at the forum,

"Look at his hands," she pointed to the outstretched smooth and un-callused marble hand of Caesar;

"The gods built all this and turned him to stone!"

"All the statues you see about you of gods or men have either come from Greece or have been made here by Greek artists; it is their quality that deceives you." I felt no little pride in my Greek heritage as I spoke.

"We shall go past one of their workshops on the way home, there you will see." I directed her up the back steps of the Curia,[3] there was no sitting that day and I thought it a good place to wait for the rain to ease. We walked down the centre aisle, past the empty raised platforms on either side where the senators sit on their folding chairs, placed there and attended by their jostling servants. She, as

---

[2] Forum: a meeting place and a market for buying and selling In this case it included slaves It was tucked away partly behind the Curia, perhaps to prevent the Vestal priests from seeing manacled slaves It was forbidden

[3] Curia: the building and the name of the assembly where the senate met Important in republican times but now lost its power to the Emperor

expected, marvelled at the polished marble facings of the walls and at the height of ceiling.

"This building reverberates with the murmur of senatorial voices, until hushed by the clear echo of the speaker, when the chamber is in session," I told her. And thought since the end of the republic the only opinion that mattered was that of the Emperor and his sycophants. With the exception of my Master, you know. The doorman opened one of the pair of huge doors at our approach; he of course, had often seen me accompanying my Master through this door on important occasions, he looked down disdainfully at my purchase.

"Just come from the forum?" He queried, with a shade of mockery in his voice and a leering disdainful grin.

"Yes." I instantly regretted coming this way. It started to rain harder and I paused at the door looking out to my left across to the temple of Julius Caesar.

"Got yourself a bargain, eh? I suppose you come through the back-way here so nobody could see her just in case they gets jealous like." His jeering, sarcastic mirth was cut short by a flash of lighting and the rumble of thunder in the heavens.

"See that?" I pulled Planets to the open door, "It came from right over Caesar's Temple to the left," I pointed, "A clear indication of divine approval, you are indeed lucky."[4] The doorman turned two shades paler, adopting his cringing tone to continue.

"I thought as soon as I saw the little miss come into the Curia, here comes a special one and I reckoned the fine upstanding and discerning gent who..."

---

[4] The Romans considered signs from the left fortuitous, to the right otherwise As she was sold in Caesar's Forum, it would seem that Caesar approved of the transaction

With a nod to Planets we walked out into the sunshine and crossed the foot of the Capitoline Hill on our right, crowned with the great Temple of Jupiter and the massive bronze statue of Nero. Awe inspiring as the temple is; it is only a copy of the Parthenon in Athens, Greece. Indeed I made it clear to Planets that all the temple architecture in Rome, is Greek in style. I am confident you approve, we have to make these things clear. We passed between the Temple of Concordia Augusta on our right and the Rostra on our left, decorated with its beaked ships:[5] the venue of many telling speeches of old; veered left around the Imperial Treasury, housed and guarded in the Temple of Saturn, the oldest temple in Rome and turned left into the Sacred Way. There were the usual assortment of youths and ne'er-do-wells, hanging about the steps along the Basilica Julia, playing board games on the grids scratched into the steps, the onlookers passing nefarious bets and half blocking the street.[6] We poor common things not having lictors,[7] we pushed our own way through the throng and suffered jostling abuse. I had to give Planets a strong warning: she was walking along the road looking around, as you would expect, with wonder and amazement, but with complete disregard to the cracks between the paving stones. I told her, it was very unlucky to tread on the cracks and only the most foolhardy or ignorant visitors do so.

"Is that why the people here take two short paces and one long one and sometimes a little hop when they walk,

---

[5] The Rostra: a speakers platform; they are usually called a 'tribuna' After Drusus won Rome's first naval victory against Antium (Anzio) in 333bc: six trophies: the bronze prows of the enemy's ships called 'Rosta' were affixed to it Later they were replaced by decorative copies

[6] Betting was illegal in ancient Rome; an injunction obeyed similarly to the modern traffic regulations

[7] Lictor: an attendant on a magistrate The number of lictors allowed depended on status They cleared a way through the mob, for the transport of their master

and with an exaggerated hip movement?" I replied a cautious "yes" to her question, but told her that,

"Some people naturally walk that way" in case she made an inappropriate inquiry into their mincing gate and the cracks, I quickly added that, "It did not apply to the army who are unconcerned about joins in the paving."

We passed under the Triumphal Arch of Augustus, appropriately adjoined on its left side to the Temple of Julius Caesar, as you know he was Caesar's adopted son. We entered the temple; I purchased grain and handed it to the priest for sacrifice before Caesar's Tomb. I prayed my gratitude to Caesar for his kindly omen and told Planets to do the same; he must be impressed that he is still remembered in Britain.[8]

Exiting from the temple I directed us between the Regia, a very old temple of Mars, converted to a house by Caesar: Caesar used it as a convenient base to direct his building works;[9] such a profanity that it caused his demise, or so some say, and the Temple of Vesta. The round form of the temple of Vesta is of course, not unfamiliar to us Greeks.

Continuing our descent along the Sacred Way, we passed the seven shops shielding the house of the Vestal Virgins, who attend the sacred flame. Also behind these shops are the College Vestal Priests. The next row of shops fronted our Master's house, not only facing along the Sacred Way, but also they continued part-way along the two side roads, perpendicular to it, forming the insular.[10] It is not a true insular, as the other end has no cross road, the two side roads terminating by abutting into the Palatine hill. The Master's garden wall continues some way up the

---

[8] Caesar first came to Britain in 55bc Then again in 54bc
[9] It is reasonable to assume that many of the edifices were erected by Emperor Augustus, Caesar's heir: in his honour
[10] Insular: an island, in this case surrounded by roads

hill, with a gate onto a private way leading to the Imperial Palace Complex, which straddles the summit.

The first shop was that of the sculptor. It occupied the large corner position with its door across the corner. It also has a removable front façade, so constructed as to easily accommodate the passage of the large blocks of marble that are the medium of this sculptor's art. I entered, followed by Planets. The master-sculptor was busy chastising one of his polishers, with vigorous buffets to the unfortunate youth's glowing reddened ear. When he had finished with the youth, he started similar administrations to his own forehead with the palm of his hand.

"Slaves, Slaves!" he repeated between thumps, "The carrier will be here shortly and he's not finished the polishing, spends all day dreaming about the girl in the bakery." He forsook his own head in favour once more of the polisher's, whack! "Look! Here, you can feel the roughness" he closed his eyes and averted his head, feeling with the little finger the inside curl of the fine marble fabric of the tunic of a prominent senator's wife. It hung gracefully about her, her shapely marble legs showing through the delicate folds of the marble fabric. The polisher redirected his Indian sand and leather buffer to the area felt by the finger.[11]

"Don't blame the boy, governor, if I spent all day polishing old mother -----'s (courtesy forbids me to give her name) varicose legs, I too would be thinking of the girl in the bakery." This aside came from an older man roughing out the side of a sarcophagus, with deft mallet and chisel work. Planets was watching him intently and saying nothing. Prudently, I surmise, staying clear of the vexed governor, who relaxed and smiled at the joke. The

---

[11] According to Pliny the elder, sand imported from India, was oxidised by heating and was used to polish marble

statue of the senator's wife was exquisite; but not so the senator's wife, it was evident she had not won the good will of the master sculptor or his crew. And how is our Master Scribe today?" Before I could open my mouth to reply, he continued,

"Your Master is my next commission he wants an exact portrait, he says, 'truth before lies, and no flattery'. I hope he values truth more than she does flattery." I had just managed the word "I" when the door opened and a burly man entered. The sculptor leaped into the air exclaiming on the thud as he landed,

"Zeus, the carriers are here now, and you boy, don't stop polishing!" he pointed to the polisher and then addressed me as he opened up a wide shutter in the front shop,

"Can't stop now, she's throwing an unveiling party, what would she do if we don't deliver?" he raised both hands to his temples at the thought, "and it's still to be painted!"

An ox cart had stopped outside; it had a low deck and a deep bed of straw. The carriers laced a soft protective deerskin around the head and body of the statue and laid it over backwards onto a blanket of hide; carefully avoiding putting pressure on the delicate protruding parts. Thus, they exited carrying the statue, stretchered between the gang of carriers, leaving the sarcophagus carver to lock up.

"Pity someone doesn't cover her over and cart her off!" muttered the sarcophagus carver, as we also exited. We watched the cart trundle along the Sacred Way, the polisher at the side, trying to apply his polish to the recumbent, jolting statue.

I noticed a Praetorian Guardsman standing in the shadows; he watched the cart pass and approached from the rear, drew his Gladius and tapped our distraught sculptor on the shoulder, as if he was testing something nasty. The sculptor jumped in the air and turned around; words passed between them with much animation resulting in the sculptor girding his clothing above his knees and legging it back to his shop. I pulled Planets into the goldsmith's shop next door. In his haste, the sculptor had forgotten his permit for a wheeled vehicle. Strict laws forbid carts in this part of Rome without a permit for the safety of the pedestrians. The gold-smith sat at his bench close to the window, he was working on a fine gold hair-net, he had it laid over a stuffed former made of stretched suede, in the shape of a head.

"What do you want? I have paid the rent, haven't I?" these questions were directed without any interruption to his work, or establishing who we were.

"I just looked in to enquire of your health" I lied.

"Oh, it's you, I am fine; now please go-away" he looked up as I ushered Planets out of the door. I refrained from entering further shops contenting myself by showing Planets their outside. The big double front doors of our house extend to the full height of the upper storey of the flanking living accommodation.

"This is the one for riding horses through," she pointed at the gleaming door of polished bronze and froze as she saw her reflection, "It's a pond on its side, how can that be?"

"It's not water its metal," I called to her. She gingerly stretched forth a hand to touch it.

"Keep your greasy fingers off," she jerked back her hand   "It speaks! It has a sprit within it."

"No that's the doorkeeper speaking through the squint," I could see he was laughing, and I was more than a little amused. I explained to the doorkeeper peering through the squint, that she was our latest purchase and I was showing her around; he raised his eyebrows and retreated into the gloom. "And this one is for the pedestrians?" Planets theorised returning to the smaller door.

"No," I corrected her "the big one is for important occasions, where important people make a grand entrance; otherwise the small one is used. Horses are not allowed in the street or the house, so important people are carried on a litter."

The other corner shop is the bakery; it has two doors, one into the street across the corner of the building, the other into the atrium, allowing access for household use. The bakery and the Sculptor's Workshop are the two biggest premises. After the bakery around the corner is the pearl and gem merchant, then for us the most important shop the Papyrus Merchant. He imports papyri prepared for writing, from Alexandria. I explained that he is not the only merchant we use and in the course of her work, she would deal with him and others. The only other shop along that side is a perfumery. I walked her back around past the big bronze doors, to the other road that bounds the insular. Planets I noticed, moved so as to keep me between her and the doors, glancing back as we went past. The first shop is a cutler, along with domestic knives he makes and repairs, he also sells spoons. Next to the cutler is a lady who specialises in embroidering clothes with gold thread. And after her a purveyor of works of literature, he sells scrolls in Latin, Greek, and Hebrew. The proprietor waved through the open window and called me in, he always liked to gossip, he probably wanted to know why I had a small barbarian in tow. I declined his offer as best I could and hurriedly pushed Planets through a small side door into the villa.

"On our right is the office, which is where you will be working," I benignly informed her.

"Yes and that is the small door, that we use," she said pointedly.

My intention had been to purchase a servant for the office scribes. One who was able to prepare the ink,[12] trim the lamp wicks and light the fire to melt the wax for the writing tablets,[13] as well as running errands and ushering in the constant stream of couriers, informers and the hopefuls looking for rewards for information from all parts of our Empire and beyond, even from India and China.

---

[12]Ink made from gum Arabic and soot or squid ink
[13]Wooden tablets have a thin layer of bees wax for writing on with a stylus By melting the wax, the tablet is rendered reusable Multiple tablets may be joined and sealed by cord through holes on the edge of the tablet, enabling them to fold together Used until medieval times

Ground Plan of Seneca's Roman Town House

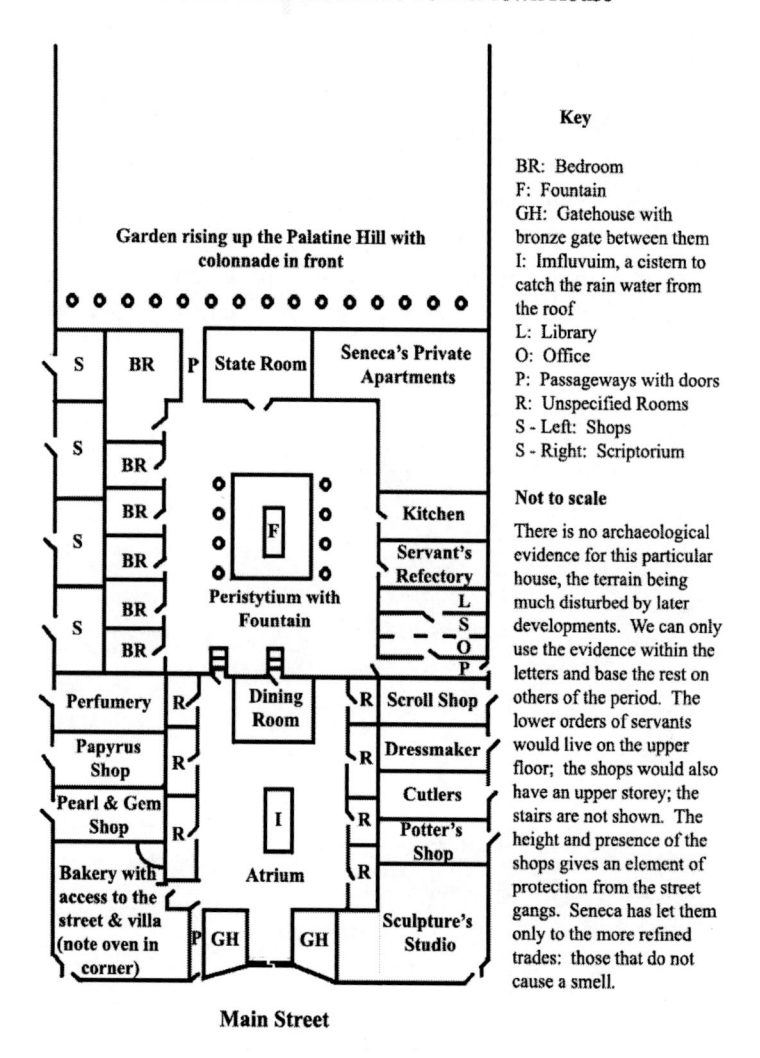

Garden rising up the Palatine Hill with colonnade in front

S	BR	P	State Room	Seneca's Private Apartments
S	BR			
	BR		F	Kitchen
S	BR			Servant's Refectory
	BR			L / S / O / P
S	BR			

Peristytium with Fountain

Perfumery	R	Dining Room	R	Scroll Shop
Papyrus Shop	R		R	Dressmaker
Pearl & Gem Shop	R	I	R	Cutlers
		Atrium	R	Potter's Shop
Bakery with access to the street & villa (note oven in corner)				
	P	GH	GH	Sculpture's Studio

Main Street

Key

BR: Bedroom
F: Fountain
GH: Gatehouse with bronze gate between them
I: Imfluvuim, a cistern to catch the rain water from the roof
L: Library
O: Office
P: Passageways with doors
R: Unspecified Rooms
S - Left: Shops
S - Right: Scriptorium

Not to scale

There is no archaeological evidence for this particular house, the terrain being much disturbed by later developments. We can only use the evidence within the letters and base the rest on others of the period. The lower orders of servants would live on the upper floor; the shops would also have an upper storey; the stairs are not shown. The height and presence of the shops gives an element of protection from the street gangs. Seneca has let them only to the more refined trades: those that do not cause a smell.

Security is paramount, as dangerous rumours are rife in Rome; they have caused many deaths of innocent men in the past. As you know, old Claudius[14] booted the Master out of Rome to Corsica. In truth, Narcissus his freedman, did the booting, old Claudius with his gammy leg, could not boot anyone, not even on the rare occasions when he was sober. He did it on the strength of a rumour spread by the Empress Messallina, that the Master was having illicit relations with Caligula's sister Julia Livilla. An unlikely rumour caused by Messallina's jealousy. Even if it were true, old Claudius must have had a soft spot for the Master, as he murdered nearly everyone else on the slightest pretext, family and senators alike. In the respect of security at least, Planets is an excellent choice, as she cannot read or write. Greek may be spoken when discussing sensitive matters, a language of which she has no knowledge.

Here in Rome, there is a standing joke that whenever a new servant or somebody of a low order, first enters the atrium of a villa that has by the front door a mosaic of a ferocious barking dog: one of the servant's barks furiously! This usually has the effect of startling the newcomer, which causes much mirth when it is pointed out that it is only a mosaic. This was tried on Planets when I showed her the front door from the inside; she looked disdainfully upon the amused gathering and said in an appalling accent,

"My home is guarded by real hounds, and where are your chickens? It's a poor home that can't afford a dog or chickens!"

---

[14] Tiberius Claudius Nero, (10bc-54ad) Became Emperor in 40ad his successor Nero, was his stepson

This made the onlookers fall about laughing, as our Master is considered the richest in Italy; but is known for his parsimony. As he says,

"I like things homely and inexpensive and food that is simple, not destined to come back by the same way it entered and not to be served by multitudes of slaves." Nevertheless, he always advocates a policy of kindness to his staff. I believe that the Master was also amused and related the dog incident to Petronius who has used it in his comedy 'The Satyricon,' written for the Emperor's[15] delectation and amusement; Nero is always fond of a comedy.

I quartered Planets with Scribonia, a widowed mother and her daughter, maidservants to the Mistress, who were to instruct Planets in the ways and manners of the household. After a week, we started to teach her the special duties of the office, allowing a month to gauge her qualities. If necessary, we could always take up the trader's offer of a part exchange deal or return her to the auction.

The widowed mother Scribonia had been in our service for six years. She sold herself with her daughter into slavery, to relieve her debts after her husband had died. He had been a trader of horses and been kicked in the leg, breaking his patella. The surgeons had amputated, but he had not acquired sufficient wealth to pay for his medical treatment. Our Mistress had discharged the debts to the surgeons, upon their enslavement and thereafter they worked in our household, attending the Mistress.

On the third day of Planets' arrival Scribonia told me how indignant Planets had been when she tried to send her cape to the laundry. When it was returned, how

---

[15] Emperor Nero, (37ad - 68ad) Became Emperor 13th October 54ad aged 16 yrs

pleased she was and clung to it like a long lost friend. Of course, this is the only possession she has and it probably substituted for the comfort of her own home. However, it did not stop her eagerly trying on her new clothes of white linen and her leather sandals. The novelty of indoor bathing was new to her, but she was always willing to search for parasites often with much success, on anyone who would sit still long enough. A service that gained her great popularity!

Never let it be said that barbarians are incapable of learning. After the next full moon she was able to execute her tasks and her Latin was not so bad either. Her simple demeanour and prompt aptitude was much admired by the scribes, even though it came as a surprise to them. Of course, scribes being scribes there are always complaints, the inks are too thin or too thick; the lamps are too smoky, or the seats are too hard. What really troubles them is that their hands cramp, their backs ache and their eyes are sore, but they don't like to admit it, these are the problems of the older scribe for fear of being sold off.

Planets' first job of the morning is to light the small charcoal stove used to melt the wax for the writing tablets. Whilst this was heating up, the leaves of the tablets were untied, in readiness for the wax to be removed, after warming over the stove, scraped off and placed in the melting pan. When the wax reaches the correct temperature, that is, just when it starts to smoke, it is poured quickly onto the tablets to make a nice smooth surface, and then cooled to receive the stylus. The tablets are stacked into neat piles on the table ready for use. When the length of the text requires more than one tablet, she would tie them together to form a hinge and then they would fold together and were kept closed with a knot, secured with a wax seal if necessary. Another task is to ensure that there are adequate supplies of soot and gum for the mixing of ink, especially when octopus ink is not available. Each scribe supplied and sharpened his own quills, appropriate to his writing style. When the papyri arrive from the merchant, Planets would examine them for evenness of texture, the correct size and weight; rejecting the defective; admonishing the merchant.

Chapter 2
Planets talks of Britain and how the Romans saved her tribe.
A meeting with the Emperor and his mistress Acte

You asked me about Britain. One evening, when alone, I asked Planets to tell me about her home. She told me that she lived by a river running at the bottom of, and between chalk hills about six miles from the sea of Gaul.[16] They lived in a roundhouse, in a group of five other roundhouses. These houses were all circular and thatched; they had trodden earth floors, with a hearth in the middle for heating and cooking; the smoke gathering in the top of the conical roof where joints of meat hung. The whole family lived together: her mother and father, a widowed aunt, their brother, his wife, one grandmother, nine children of various ages and two slaves who worked on the farm; also there were, chickens, guard dogs and sundry orphaned kids, lambs and calves, all under the same roof.

Planets told me how all the community would worship their gods on the special March festive day, a preparatory time before sowing, when the sap was rising and willows were in full bud. All the family went down between the fields to the path by the river, to meet their neighbours and await the arrival of the people from higher up the valley. They formed a line each person holding at arms length, the waist of the person in front. As they proceeded they walked in time to the rhythm of a hymn suited to the season, the chanting of which was broken by

---

[16] The English Channel

the joyful salutations when awaiting families joined the procession. The family who, on that occasion, had the honour to provide the sacrificial rams, always took precedence at the head of the procession leading the victims,[17] otherwise they all joined the tail.

Thus, they proceeded along the line of the riverbank eventually coming to a grove of oak trees concealing a circular clearing within and entered the woody confines. Constructed opposite the entrance and between two large oak trees was a high bench. Seated there, were three Matrons. Above them, a great oaken carved panel depicted the scene below: three Matrons, this time bearing unruly infants about their persons.[18] The women on the bench had achieved their position by being the progenitors of the most grandchildren, and represented fecundity, family, health and food. Consequently, they were the three mothers most blessed by the deities whose likeness was carved above them and consulted on all matters of importance. The sacrificial fire had been prepared in the centre of the clearing the day before.

It had been lit at daybreak, about one hour before the procession arrived to allow it to get hot and not too smoky, cauldrons of water had been set over the fire to heat. Barrels of ale were also placed around for the convenient filling of jugs.

When the procession arrived, the leading family with their victims took up the prominent position in front of the fire, opposite the three Matrons. The rest moved around the fire, so they could all be heard and witness the proceedings, filling their jugs as they did so. When all had assembled the three Matrons stood up and asked the

---

[17] Sacrificial rams
[18] A similar depiction in stone was found at Cirencester, and is displayed in the Corinivm Museum

deities to bless all the people present and accept the first offering of ale, they solemnly poured their ale onto the ground. The rest then chanted,

"Please accept this offering," and poured their ale onto the ground. All the gathering then recharged their jugs and with the words:

"Good health to the golden corn," and emptied the ale down their throats, with much satisfaction!

The three Matrons then sat down and asked,

"Is there any business?"

At this signal, proposed marriage contracts were announced and permission was sought by the young men to join the army of Cogidubnus,[19] in the hope of winning renown and glory by fighting alongside of the second Legion Augusta. Also, all other enterprises affecting the community were to be announced, sometimes attracting objections particularly over land claims.

The two rams were now hoisted onto the gallows sited near the Matrons' bench and hung there, by the hobbles attached to their hind legs. Now, in complete silence at a signal given by the Matrons, the belly of the first victim was slit open, the entrails tumbled out spreading onto the ground before the Matrons, who studied the victim's gyrations closely before turning their attention to the other victim. The same procedure followed. They now descended from their elevated bench and squeezed, smelt and rubbed various parts of the prostrate entrails. Conferring, they returned to the bench and ordered the slaughter of the still living victims, this was executed with a deft cut to the jugular. As the blood gushed forth, two appointed maids dashed forward to catch the precious liquid in oaken bowls. These bowls

---

[19] Cogidubnus, King of the Atrebates ally of Rome

were passed from one Matron to the other, who sucked the still warm blood in to their mouths and then all the maidens went up to each matron in turn who passed the precious liquid from her own mouth, into to the maid's upturned mouth for her to swallow. Their future fertility was now assured. Planets was at the time too young to receive this rite. I reassured her, that now in Rome when the time came, she too would be touched by Flora's herb.[20] Now each farmer knelt at the Matrons' feet who anointed them with the blood by making a mark of a phallus on his forehead and receiving a blessing for their crops.

Rising murmurs of the expectant onlookers was hushed by a gesture of the senior Matron's hand. By the evidence of the augury previously witnessed, the Matrons adjudicated and advised. Each judgment was followed by the praise of approval or disappointment of the concerned parties. The carcasses were now butchered; the offal and brains and small joints were put into the cauldrons of boiling water, the other meat being spit-roasted. The slaughter, butchery and cooking was carried out by the family responsible for supplying the victims.

The most bold adolescent girls, after refreshing themselves with beer, started to dance around the fire to the enthusiastic clapping of their elders, soon the shyer ones joined them after drinking a little more of the beer. Watching keenly how gracefully or otherwise these maidens performed. Mothers would select prospective wives for their sons, whilst their sons watched keenly. After a while the sons were invited to join the dance, usually with a shove from their mothers, who observed to whom they where attracted; often with disappointment.

---

[20] Flora: an ancient Goddess of flowers and fertility Flora gave Juno a magic herb the touch of which caused Juno to give birth to Mars

Following this, the whole congregation joined in rounds of drinking, singing and dancing until it was feast time. Infants and the young received the offal and brains, as these were considered the most nutritious and easily digested parts, the adults feasted on the flesh, whilst the dogs feasted on the bones. Those who were able made their way home, the rest slept on the ground where they could, with complete indifference to the weather.

Planets observed that, talking of food and drink caused her to feel hungry and thirsty, it was now past our mealtime. So we went to the servants refectory and there provisioned ourselves with bread and cheese, wine and water. It is my rule that food and drink is not permitted in the office: the risk of damage to the papyri must be kept to the minimum. I therefore took her to my private chamber, it being the only place where we would not be disturbed. She lay on my bed, whilst I sat on the chair by my desk. During our meal, I asked her what she knew of the past, before she was born. While she was talking, I could not help being distracted by the strands of her loosened hair spread out over my pillow and the smooth purity of her light skin in the soft glow of the oil lamp.

She looked at me and smiled, then continued. Telling me how, when she was younger, during the long winter evenings the men would sit close to the light of the fire in the roundhouse, carving wood or bone tools and trinkets. The girls and women, when not feeding babies, spent their time spinning wool. As they carved and spun, they would talk about the old days when the Lord Verica travelled to Rome to secure the aid of the Roman Legions from the Emperor Claudius. How their enemies the 'Catuvellauni'[21]

---

[21] Catuvellauni: a tribe with its heartland in Essex Following is an account of the Roman invasion of 43ad

would ride their horses and chariots along the tracks and through the great wood to the North causing great alarm amongst the people.[22] Everybody fleeing before them, as the alarm spread, driving all the livestock they had time to round up, trying to reach the safety of the defensive lines around Noviomagvs.[23] On their return, all creatures with legs had been driven off; the human kind in chains to be sold into slavery in the north, some being traded across the sea to lower Germany, and along the Rhine and Elbe. If they were lucky, sometimes the grain hidden away in secret storage pits may have survived the raids, providing that a captive or a disloyal slave had not revealed its whereabouts. The Catuvellauni were a fearsome tribe, who knew how to discover secrets from their captives.

This part of the story was accompanied with deep groans and wailings from the rest of the family, the story teller pausing to wipe away his tears, as he talked of the burning. The raids steadily got worse until the Roman God and Emperor Claudius landed his army in the territory of the Cantiaci,[24] on the far east of the south coast and marched inland towards the Catuvellauni's heartland.

A vexillation[25] of legionaries had already landed in Noviomagvs[26] to help with the defence; their gods proved invincible. When the Catuvellauni retreated from Noviomagvs, all followed the Centurion's advice and waited behind the defences in case they counter attacked. However, when the news of the invasion came from the East, it was clear that the Catuvellauni were fast retreating north to defend their homes! At this point the listeners

---

[22] The Sussex Weald

[23] These defences are visible today, to the North of Chichester

[24] Cantiaci: a tribe in Kent The main Roman force landed on the Isle of Thanet, Kent

[25] Vexillation: a part of a legion on other duties

[26] Noviomagvs: Now Chichester, Sussex

would abandon their spinning or carving and jump up and down, cheering and shouting war cries; treading on various infants and chickens and falling on the fire. The story teller shouted excitedly above the din: 'Now it is our turn to ride through the great wood and attack their rear!' Everybody in the round house who could and some who should not, having drunk the strong beer, leaped into the air brandishing make-do weapons (the smaller creatures retreated to the periphery.) Men from all over the south joined forces under the banner of our new king Cogidubnus fighting with the glorious Second Augusta Legion. The kingdom was regained; the Atrebates recovered their old city of Caleva.[27]

When the Master and I were suffering in exile in Corsica, the Master was corresponding with Claudius's freedman, Narcissus, who at that time was effectively administrating the Empire. Narcissus masterminded the strategy and organised the invasion of Britain, using the information given to him earlier by the British Lord Verica.[28] The reason for the invasion to the east and not through the beleaguered Atrebates kingdom was that by attacking the Catuvellauni homeland north of the Temes, by following the line of the Temes Estuary,[29] would force them into a hurried retreat to defend their crops, livestock and to save families from enslavement by cutting off the invading Legions.

According to Planets, this is exactly what happened. Of course, the countryside of the Atrebates remained free of the ravages of war, stayed loyal, and remains a valuable

---

[27] Caleva: Silchester near Reading, Berkshire, to become an important city on the crossing of the road system
[28] A new letter the writer tells what he knows of the invasion of Briton (43ad) Verica was Cogidubnus' predecessor
[29] The Thames Estuary

supplier of meat and grain to the army. Narcissus boasted how he had to stiffen up the Legions morale when Commander Aulus Plautius and the Legions lost their nerve before embarking at Boulogne. He did this by haranguing them for their cowardice and appealing to their greed by extolling the wealth they could attain by simply crossing a stretch of water. Planets was amused when I told her this, as she thought Britain was poorer than Gaul and mostly noted by the legionaries for its damp weather, causing weapons and armour to rust.

Of course, Narcissus spoke as a surrogate of old Claudius, who had kept himself safely in Rome, his stammer restricting his oration to the nod of the head. On certain judicial occasions, Claudius would be examining a hapless individual, when the executioner would misinterpret a nod, as old Claudius also had an involuntary tic of the head, and order the arrest of the victim for the chop, to the extreme protestations of a panicking innocent victim. I remember an occasion when a lucky talisman fell from the clothing of a successful advocate from Gaul, it was a painted egg. It was impossible to know from Claudius' reaction, whether he was reprimanding or congratulating the advocate for taking all precautions to gain an acquittal; Claudius had stuttered in bad Greek. The unfortunate advocate was eagerly whisked off on the strength of an imperial nod and executed. The guilty defendant allowed to go free.

The Gallic sea had acquired a fearsome reputation for storms and monsters, following Germanicus' disastrous naval operations on the Rhine Estuary seventeen years before, when a great storm drove the fleet out to sea. The few survivors that washed up on the north east coast of Britain eventually returned, with wild stories of primitive tribes, sea monsters and giant birds. Over the years these stories told in the brothels and taverns, had had their effect on the minds of the common soldiers. Although, a great Roman victory in Britain was claimed by Claudius and Aulus Plautius, the real architect of the invasion was like me, a freed Greek slave and the whole Empire knew it; but kept quiet! Old Claudius did cross to Britain, but the Elephants he took with him died on crossing when the ship capsized. Claudius stayed in the south well away from the fighting; but claimed a victory for himself upon his quick return to Rome.

Planets was having difficulty in keeping her eyes open, sleepily telling me how, in the peace after the invasion, the farmers were able to improve their livestock and started to breed larger sheep by importing rams from the distant parts of the Empire through the trade routes that were now available to them. Greater wealth was attained by the demand for flesh and grain to supply the Legions. Some of these provisions were paid for, but others were collected as taxes, for the King. These were the good times. After the men returned from the stock drives to Noviomagvs, they would tell of how a new town was growing there, with square buildings of flint walls, held together miraculously with cement,[30] and of new temples with columns and courtyards. Outside the town, industries were set up near the stockyard, there cattle were slaughtered, salted and packed into barrels; winter rations for the Legions. The hides were cleaned and dried ready for the tanners. On the Strand, shipwrights repaired and constructed the ships that traded to Gaul, the Rhine and along the coast, east and west. To the east of the town in the quiet and less smelly country, a great new palace was being constructed for the use of the royal family in the

---

[30] Cement: a Roman invention, unknown in Britain until the invasion

style of a Country Roman villa;[31] larger than the palace Planets was now living in. The engineers of the second Legion worked on this building, also on the construction of a new road across the hills, to the King's second town of Caleva. This work was carried out during the winter when the campaigning season had ended; using slaves gained by their many victories in the north and west. She just managed to say in a tired hushed whisper,

"They thought it was a great marvel to us and a boon, as it relieved the need for travel along our valley," then she fell quiet: Morpheus had relieved her of the conscious day. I moved the lamp closer to write my notes. When I had finished and rested my stylus, I looked down; she was lying on her side with her thumb in her mouth. Stupid of me I know, I should have sent her to her own bed, but I remember turning my chair towards the bed, resting my feet there, blowing out the lamp and staying awake: it was uncomfortable.

The following day, grave news arrived from Gaul.[32] Catus Declanus the Imperial Agent had fled Britain following a revolt of all the tribes. He had managed to escape at the last moment with the tax money he had collected for the Emperor. Had the new Imperial Governor, Gaius Suetonious Paulinus suffered the fate of Varus after he crossed the Rhine? Were Roman heads now displayed on stakes before the jeering victors as they stamped Imperial Eagles into the Roman gore?[33] It appeared that the whole province had been lost. Burrus,[34]

---

[31] A large number of animal bones including dog bones have been found outside the Eastgate of Chichester

[32] The Boudicca revolt, confirms the date of this letter to 60-61ad

[33] A reference to Publius Quinctilius Varus' loss of three legions, when ambushed in the Teutoburger Forest, Germany 9ad He committed suicide

[34] Sextus Afranius Burrus died 62ad Commander of the Praetorian Guard and with Seneca was the major influence on the young Emperor Nero

as head of the Imperial Guard, had received this information and passed it on to our Master. The Master summoned myself and Planets into his presence, to ascertain Planets' opinion and to warn her that her tribe, the Atrebates, might have been either decimated or deserted to the rebels. Planets did not believe it possible that the Atrebates would abandon the Second Legion Augusta. They had long been devoted allies, supplying its cavalry with support and provisions, her own father had ridden in support of them. The Master ordered the household to offer prayers to Mars for the Legions and not to show any animosity to Planets, as her people might have suffered in the rebellion. We cancelled all business for the day. I asked her if there was a Deity she would like to make a sacrifice to.

"Leven is our god of healing, we deposit wax or wooden effigies of the afflicted part, person or animal in his stream and as they drift away so the malady heals. But I used to go down and listen to him talking in his gurgling language, and he listened to my whispered pleas and allowed me to come here".

"We could sacrifice to Minerva" I suggested that she is popular in Rome and will listen with a favourable ear.

"Thank you", she said, "but I will only ask Minerva to safeguard my parents".

That evening I retired early to bed to catch up on my lack of sleep of the previous night. She had not seemed strongly perturbed about the possible fate of her kinsmen. Curiosity demanded that I should discover more of her past.

The following morning, she was not busying herself in the office as usual. My enquiries resulted in Scribonia telling me that, during the night, she had been summoned along with the Master into the presence of Nero. An

Emperor's summons can result in anything between being laden with riches or an execution by the cruellest means devised by man, I was rather alarmed.

"Is she all right?" I hastily enquired.

"Yes, she is fine, just had a late night, I will get her up and send her to you in the office".

I now had even more to ask her. Planets entered the office and went to prepare the stove.

"We have not got time for that now, come and tell me about your escapade last night. We'll go to my chamber!"

"But who will look after my scribes today?" she said.

"Today, the scribes can look after themselves! I want to know what the Emperor said"

The scribes did not look at all pleased, they also to wanted to know what the Emperor had wanted. I noticed how she regarded them familiarly as her scribes. We took up our former position, her on my bed and I at the desk.

"Now tell me what happened last night!"

"Last night, I was awakened by Scribonia, who told me to dress in clean clothes as the Master wanted to see me and was waiting in the peristylium by the fountain.[35] She had no idea what for, but urged me to hurry. The Master told me that the Emperor wanted to see me; he knew I was from Britain, and wanted to know what the British looked like. The Master had informed Nero about me earlier and my opinions on the rebellion. Presumably, he wanted to question me about them himself. Nero often has whims during the night and the best that he could advise was that I should always pay attention to what he said and answer with courtesy, caution and never criticism. I did not feel too alarmed, as I thought he could not be worse than my grandmother. I walked behind the

---

[35] Peristylium: an open space in the centre of the villa, beyond the atrium

Master with the lamp bearers in front and close behind along the garden and through a gate in the back wall."

"That's the private way into the palace" I interjected.

"Yes, it led up the Palatine hill and up steps into the palace; guards saluting as we passed. We waited in the ante- chamber, to be ushered in. I noticed how splendid the servants looked in their embroidered robes trimmed with gold, and thought, how different from the round-houses at home with their mud daubed walls is this huge building, with its walls of shiny marble; the Emperor must be even more splendid.

The usher then announced us as 'Lucius Annaeus Seneca and Slave'.[36] To my surprise, the Master walked over to a rather scruffy looking youth, discoursing with a lady some years older, reclining on a couch and eating a small bird offering pieces to their companions. She was dressed in a stola,[37] with an ornate necklace, bracelet and earrings to match. In her thick dark hair she wore pearls; her lips were as red as cherries. Opposite, reposed several young courtly men, attired in togas edged with embroidery. They seemed to be paying attention to the scruffy one. Behind them stood attendants with jars of wine, ready, instantly to refill any emptied glass goblets; others equally richly attired, attended to the food bringing it from a table as required on platters of silver inlaid with gold. Some of the attendants were assisting one of the young men to vomit into a bucket, wiping his face when he had finished and mopping up the vomit which had

---

[36] Annaeus Seneca 3bc – 65ad Studied philosophy, was influenced by the Cynics Claudius banished him to Corsica however, in 49ad Agrippina recalled him to Rome to become praetor and tutor to Nero her son He is referred to by the writer as his Master

[37] Stola: a ladies full length garment made from either fine linen or coarser fabric depending on person's status, and worn over the tunic

missed the bucket and splattered over his clean white toga, feet and the mosaic floor.

"Seneca my friend and tutor, is this the one you talked of earlier?" Nero said in a slightly slurred voice. The Master answered,

"Yes sir, this is the one from Britain".

I was surprised at him being the Emperor as he was the worst dressed in the room. Wearing a dark tunic that was none too clean! However, he did have a diadem on his head! He stood up walked around me a little unsteadily and told me to sit where he had been sitting, next to the lady with the jewellery. She patted the cushion and gave a smile. The Master had stepped back out of the way.

The Emperor faced me, and regarding me thoughtfully said,

"Do you like music?"

"I liked it when at home spinning, we used to sing songs".

"Well, I'll sing you a song, my own words, composed it this morning" he said, and with that he took up a strange instrument and told me,

"This is a lyre, see how you like it".

It was actually very pleasant and I listened closely as he plucked the strings and turned knobs. When he had finished, they all clapped with rapt enthusiasm, I noticed what they did and I clapped too. He turned to the others acknowledging their applause and said, "There you are; now its tuned I'll sing you a song".

I preferred the lyre tuning, but the song was all right and I clapped with the rest. The Emperor laid down the lyre and hushed the applause with a downward stoke of the hand and proclaimed,

"Seneca, all is not lost in Britain! As you have just witnessed, the people of the Atrebate at least appreciate the artistic brilliance of their Emperor, unlike some Romans, and therefore could not have been part of the rebellion. Britain will be saved!"

Nero asked me if I liked my relatives.

"No" I said, "I don't like them at all!"

"And I didn't like mine" he said very pleased, "I think Britain will prosper more than Britannicus."[38] Everyone laughed and clapped! He then introduced me to the lady sitting next to me, saying "This is Acte; she was once a slave like you, now would you like another song?"

I agreed and Acte gave me a honeyed walnut. When he finished, he announced to the young men that it was now time to go out, telling his companions to dress for the occasion like himself. They left his presence and he went over to Acte, gesticulating to us both to rise. As she did so, I noted her long stola concealed that she, in a short while, would produce a child. He kissed her and patted me on the head. Then said to her,

"See that this slave is given some decent clothing to wear, not the measly stuff Seneca prefers for his household. And look after this!" he rubbed her on the belly.

"Now we shall go!" he addressed the others who had returned dressed similarly to himself in scruffy tunics. When they left, the Master told Acte to leave me dressed as I was, otherwise, I would arouse the jealousy of the rest of his household. Acte agreed with him, much to my disappointment. And that is all that happened. Can I have a drink?"

---

[38] Britannicus: Claudius' natural son was supplanted by Nero when Claudius adopted Nero as his heir, the son of Agrippina his second wife He suffered from fits and choked during a meal; Nero was present and is thought to have poisoned him

I was relieved; it seemed that Nero had gone off on one of his jaunts to the seedier parts of Rome, to banter with the pimps and prostitutes in the streets and taverns. Acte as always had followed the Master's instruction and Planets had not said a wrong word. Although she could not have understood Nero's joke, he had poisoned his stepbrother Britannicus, a necessity to safely secure his position. It was fortunate that he had not referred to Planets' mother, as the fate of his own mother caused him to be morose and unpredictable.

I poured two glasses of watered wine. After we both drank, I broached the question of why Planets' family showed animosity towards her. Her mother had told her that, on the day of her birth, her aunt had also given birth to a stillborn child. On the same day she also received news that her husband had died when his horse stumbled throwing him off, to die not in battle, but herding sheep, was considered by many to be a disgrace more than a misfortune. . From this time on, her aunt always held a grudge against Planets and her mother, although younger than her sister, had more children. To make matters worse, her fractious aunt had no more children, no other men had shown interest in marrying her; she had to be content with the services of the slave; an old one at that. She never lost an opportunity to cause trouble for Planets. One evening in the round house, when Planets was playing with her favourite puppy, the aunt was so enraged that she snatched up the puppy, and threw it on the fire! The smell of the burning fur and the flaming puppy caused a panic for the door, preventing Planets' escape. The aunt used the opportunity to beat her around the head with a stick. Whilst her grandmother shouted,

"That'll teach the brat to pay us proper respect!"

"Grandmother did not like you, either?" I said.

"No, mother told me that the aunt blamed me for her subsequent barrenness and grandmother as a consequence, would never have sufficient grandchildren to become a Matron and preside at the fertility rites. Thus, those two elder women both blamed me for their problems and shame. Then some of the sheep started behaving strangely: running with a high step, scratching the wool from their sides, shaking and then standing still gazing at the stars. After a while they died![39]

Special models were carved of the sheep, with their strange characteristics. The shepherds placed these in the river in order that Leven, who lived in the river[40] and manifested himself along the misty banks, would take pity and return the sheep to normal. As more sheep succumbed to the malady, people started saying that Leven was affronted by my eye and that is the reason why the sheep were staring at the stars. One night, my father gently aroused me told me to pick up my cape and quietly leave the roundhouse. I could feel my mother sobbing and her tears wet my face as she held me tight, for the last time. We slowly walked away from the sleeping farms, my father and I, to where his pony was tethered, he lifted me into the saddle and led us on a slow walk towards Noviomagvs. On the way he explained that if I stayed at home my aunt or grandmother would have roused up the community to have me killed. The safest place for me was out of the country. He had arranged with a trader to take me to Rome to be sold into a fine household. I was to learn to speak Latin; this he thought would not be difficult for me, being the cleverest girl in the land.

---

[39] This sounds like Scrapie In cattle this is known as mad cow disease This may affect humans who ingest the brains of infected animals as apparently occurring at the sacrificial feast

[40] The river Levant: Leven being the Deity locus

When Noviomagvs came into sight, he stopped, we both sat with our backs resting against a tree, there was no need to hurry as the ship was waiting for the tide. He explained how sad he was to lose me and was sorry that he had been unable to save me from the violence at home. Had I been a boy I could have proved my worth in the saddle, away from the women. Reluctantly, we moved off past the town with its new buildings and onto the strand. There, bobbing about a little way off in the lapping water, was moored the ship, with the trader pacing the strand. We headed towards him.

"This is my girl," my father said, "She is clever and learns quickly."

"Well get her off the pony and into the boat, the tide is turning and it waits for no man!" the trader was impatient, a small leather boat as long as a man was ready to carry us to the ship. My father lifted me from the pony into the boat with hands he was previously using to wipe away his silent tears and tried to give me a reassuring smile. The trader gave father a sum of money.

He gave it back to the trader saying,

"This is to make sure she is treated well and learns Latin". Those were the last words I heard him utter. He mounted the pony and rode away; we rowed to the ship, I watched his back, he didn't look round and soon the fierce tide was drawing the ship out of the harbour."

The wine jug was now empty. I said to Planets,

"We should now cheer ourselves up."

"I was never sad," she said defiantly, "Like Nero I was glad to see the back of them. The best thing dad ever did for me." She went on to tell me that the ships cargo was mostly local salt beef packed in barrels. One barrel though, contained a roll of hooded capes, like Planets' cape, made from wool gathered from the sheep that graze the grassy hills around Noviomagvs, closely woven, boiled and beaten to a form felt. They sailed past the shallow saltpans, where captured brine evaporated in the summer sun leaving a crust of white salt.

"I felt wonderful breathing in the fresh sea air, feeling the ship come alive, free of my people, free of my troubles; although now a slave. It only lasted until we cleared the harbour and got out to sea; then I was sick. As I leaned over the side, the crew enquired with their customary maritime jocularity, if I was bowing to Neptune or feeding fish. Upon my recovery they explained that the ship was lightly loaded, causing it to lurch about in the choppy water, they urged me to keep up the bowing as they had favourable weather and were making good progress. The next time the ship lurched, I had no difficulty complying with their request. By sunset, we had passed through the channel between Vectis Inis[41] and the mainland, further on entered another large harbour on the rising tide and moored alongside a jetty on the western foreshore."[42] I stopped her there as I had more than enough notes to write up.

---

[41] Isle of Wight
[42] Poole Harbour or Hengistbury head

Chapter 3
Planets' adventures leaving Britain. The murder of the city prefect. Acte makes a plea for her baby. Cinnamus talks of Paul of Tarsus.

Burrus had sent a centurion of the Praetorian Guard, to arrest Catus Decianus[43] or more importantly in Nero's view, to secure the money he had with him when he fled Britain. Rumours of the British catastrophe had spread around Rome. Blame was apportioned to the mystical religions from the east that had gained popularity in the Empire. Mythras in particular had penetrated the army; Mars was not pleased and the Jews still refused to allow statues of the Imperial family to be set up in their temples.

An old Jewish acquaintance[44] of my youth at Tarsus has come to Rome, under Roman protection for arousing dissention in the Jewish community. They objected to his pro-Roman attitude; one's actions, he teaches, are paramount to righteousness: gods care not if there are statues in the temple, they are only stone; and why would he create man in his perfect image and then demand that they snip bits off? His father, I remember, supplied tents to the army. We both would stand with the other youths at the feet of the teachers and the philosophers in the forum at Tarsus. Although a Pharisee he was always daydreaming and showed an interest in the Gnostics, I think he suffered from fits.

---

[43] Catus Decianus a provincial procurator This letter although a subject change, seems to fit in here

[44] Paul of Tarsus: St Paul These references are probably the reason for the survival of the letters

It was two days later before I had time to continue my enquiry into Planets' past.

"Olondus the Merchant of Narbo was the name of the trader; my new owner." Planets told me as we walked to my room and took up our usual positions, I vowed to myself not to let her fall asleep, as she related her story. After pouring out the wine and making herself comfortable, she continued.

"Olondus left the ship telling me to stay with the crew, returning shortly with another man. They sampled wine poured from the remaining amphora that had been left on the ship; the others having been sold at Noviomagvs.

"I'll take the last four. Who's the girl?" he said looking at me, "she is a bit scraggy. Do you want to throw her in with the deal?"

"No, she's bound for the Roman market where I can get the best price for her; I will fatten her up on the way."

They looked me up and down doubtfully.

"Now let's look at the iron; and talk money." said Olondus, as they both walked back to the shore and there, examined a pile of what turned out to be iron blooms. I watched them fervently gesticulating at the blooms, the boat and the heavens; writing calculations on a flat stone with a piece of chalk. Finally spitting on their hands and clasping them to secure a deal. I hoped I was not a part of it! Coins were exchanged.

Olondus returned to the ship, the other person entered a small roundhouse and emerged followed by six other slaves in pairs, with their feet chained together. A seventh followed them with a whip. Each slave picked up four iron blooms in an orderly fashion supervised by the seventh man with the aid of his whip! They carried them in file to the ship's side and passed them to the crew one at a time, who carefully arranged them in the ships hull, placing them on staves of wood and securing them together. The four remaining amphora of wine were unloaded and carried back to the roundhouse by the slaves. I stayed where I was in the ship. I noticed that these slaves were young, lean and downcast; their blue tattooed bodies bearing scars of battle and of the whip and the shackles. This business was concluded in time for us to catch the ebbing tide; to carry us, once more into the wide ocean. Olondus was pleased with the deal and the quick turn around. He told me that the slaves were captured warriors, defeated in battle and never would have the opportunity like me, to see the great city of Rome; only to feel the oppression of hard labour.

We continued our westerly course, the ship had, as they said, 'settled further into the water' I did no more bowing to Neptune. Olondus produced a folded writing tablet from his leather satchel. He made up his accounts noting how much money he had and the quantity of cargo.

Then he turned to me:

"Now," he said, "Your ability to learn Latin will directly affect your value, and your value affects your treatment. You don't want to end up like the slaves you've just seen. Believe me, you'll be better off in a rich man's house living a life of luxury, but this can only happen if your Latin is good enough."

I needed little encouragement,

"When can we start?"

"Now" he said, "We start today and each day we do a little more."

That is how I learnt my Latin. I found it quite easy to learn and used it as much as possible in conversation with the ships company.

The wide ocean is not the empty place you would expect it to be. Although, you can't always see land there are plenty of things to look at. There are masses of white birds that dive into the sea after fish, and make a lot of noise when doing so. There are big fish that swim along in front of the ship, leaping out of the water and crashing back into it again and big moving islands that occasionally spout water. The sailors trailed lines with baited hooks on them in the wake from our stern, to catch the bright silver blue skinned mackerel. These were cooked over the ship's fire, and were eaten with relish by the whole Company and washed down with good Noviomagvs' ale. Olondus told me that he had to get special permission from the ship's owner-captain to allow me on board as he makes it a rule not to take slaves as a cargo. The captain joked that they are too troublesome, having to be shackled to the ship to prevent them from overcoming the crew and sailing home. However, he considered I was too puny to be much of a threat. Also, they have to be fed and watered, to say nothing of putting up with their complaints.

As the captain said "Cargo that doesn't walk or talk is best!"

And, I thought, a cargo that won't be sick!

I asked them how they knew which way to steer the ship when they could not see the land. The captain told me that, he had learnt as a boy from his uncle how to navigate by the position of the sun as it moved across the sky in daytime and by the stars at night. He said, that after a few trips you get the feel for the water, the currents the wind, and the smell of the land, and that ability is passed on from generation to generation. His people, who came from the Gironde, had been sailing this trade route from before the time of Julius Caesar's conquest of Gaul.[45]

"But what happens at night when there are no stars shining?" I asked.

"You can tell by the wind direction and the look of the sea," he said. "But the worst things are sudden gales, these can catch you out and many a ship has been lost. That is why all sons do not accompany their fathers and brothers in the same ship, as that way whole families are lost."

The following day we sighted land to the north, which meant we were halfway to our next destination. In a few hours time they said,

"We have to be very careful to avoid a small island, which is directly on our course."

Before we approached this island, a crewmember was ordered to the top of the main mast to keep a look out, he jested,

"You can keep watch on both me and the island, at the same time, Verriculla"

A remark that reminded me of home but without the spite; we safely sailed to the north of it,[46] and continued steadily westwards.

They struck the mainsail leaving the smaller one under the raked bowsprit and slowed the ship. They wanted to approach the next harbour on the incoming tide, after careful consideration the captain ordered full sail, we entered a wide harbour 'the land of the Dvmnonii, the land of tin' I was told.

---

[45] Gaius Julius Caesar 100 – 44bc conqueror of Gaul (France) invaded Britain twice and withdrew, founder of the Julian Dynasty Nero was the last The captain was of the tribe of the Santoni
[46] Eddystone Rocks

It had a rocky shore with cliffs and wooded valleys coming down to the sea. The trees were already changing their leaves to autumn hues.

There were no salt pans here, no white chalk, no expanse of ooze; but it was still beautiful, not quite as beautiful as Noviomagvs' harbour I think. We passed the mouths of two large creeks the first on the east the second on the south and then two more opposite each other, they were smaller but our main channel was still a good mile wide. The captain took the steering oar and set it over to take us in towards the west shore. We came very close to the rocky bank, suddenly with an extra men on the steering oar, it was pulled hard round and the mainsail loosened to spill wind; we entered a narrower channel, all done on the captain's command. Olondus congratulated the captain on 'a nifty turn on the eddy'.[47] Past the entrance and round the bend, the creek broadened but as it went further, it narrowed and divided; we sailed slowly up the northern channel with a full sail set, as inland the wind had reduced to whisper. The smell of smouldering oak smoke told us of the settlement ahead.

It was just a few small round houses with a small boat like our tender and another longer and thinner, this one hewn from the bole of an oak tree.[48] The channel had narrowed, and with the sail struck, the ship was eased to its mooring with slow sweeps of the steering oar.

We were greeted by the family of fisher folk who lived there. Our mooring rope was thrown to the bank and secured to a thorn tree before the settlement The steering oar on the side of the ship was removed before

---

[47] He used the eddy caused by incoming tide to assist the entry into Restronguet Creek

[48] A coracle and a dugout canoe; different boats for different purposes The skin clad coracle is not good around rocks, but better on mud

disembarking; allowing the ship to keel over on its side when the outgoing tide left the ship high and dry.

I was given a small basket and told to collect blackberries and to make sure I returned before dark. They need not have worried about that, two of the crew had purchased a brace of fowl from the fisherman's family and were now preparing a fire on the flat gravel above the high water mark, food for me has a strong allure, particularly after being at sea.

Blackberries are plentiful in the late summer. In a short time I returned with a filled basket. They called me over and told me to dig a hollow in the gravel close to the fire, line it with dock leaves and fill it up with as many blackberries as I could find. All the time, as I progressed back and forth between the blackberry bush and the blackberry dump, I noticed the progress of the meal. Firstly, they got a good fire going with a stock of firewood from the fisherman, there was plenty of gorse and that makes a good fire. A sizable pot of fresh water had been placed on the fire, taken from the small burn that trickled into the creek, cutting little channels through the gravel at low tide. While the cooks waited for the fire to heat up and disperse the smoke, they sat cross-legged preparing the fowl, feathers flying about in all directions.

The water there had a far more earthy taste than our water at home. Obviously, this is due to the different Deity who inhabits this burn. I felt the chill of the evening as dusk encroached and grew apprehensive in case the unknown deity objected to my fruit gathering activities. Kneeling on the bank I offered a little prayer asking who ever he might be, not to be angry, and take pity on me, and also my comrades and master, 'although I am but a homeless slave' and accept this little offering of blackberries. I made a cup for the fruit with my two hands, placing them in the water, allowing them to run out between my fingers. A lightning blue flash of a kingfisher signalled the acceptance of my offering; I smiled to myself with satisfaction.

We all gathered around the light of the fire holding our wooden plates in anticipation. A thick porridge of oats and goats cream had been cooked, laced with plenty of blackberries and apples from the fisherman's orchard. A bed of this porridge was spread on our plates, with succulent pieces of the spit roast fowl laid on top and garnished with a sauce of raw blackberries.

During the serving of the meal, a disagreement arose over the correct protocol. It was agreed that the captain should be served first, followed by Olondus the trader; he clamed that I should be served next as he owned me and therefore I was a part of him, whose position had precedence over the rest of the crew. The crew disputed this, arguing that, as I was a slave and they plebeians, clearly it was their turn next. Their indignation amused the Captain and Olondus who willingly conceded the point.

That night we slept in one of the small round houses on beds of bracken, a plant not found in my own district, it is very comfortable, especially after trying to sleep on the hard ship's poop-deck.[49] Nobody arose early that morning the sun was quite high when I set out for a morning walk."

I had to cut Planets' story short; there was a message at the door; I was summoned to the master concerning the affair of the terrible murder of the City Prefect, Lucius Pedanius Secundus, by one of his slaves.[50] Burrus'

---

[49] Poop-deck: rear deck of a ship stood on by the steers-man This ship is partly decked fore and aft

[50] The Roman historian Tacitus puts this incident at a later date

investigation of the household servants revealed under torture, that the murderer had a lover, a fellow slave,[51] described as a pretty youth, with a soft firm body, sweet breath and golden curly hair. Prefect Pedanius coveted him and quite within his rights forced him to give carnal gratification. He then conceitedly enquired of the youth, 'Who makes the better lover, Pedanius the City Prefect or the common slave his lover?' The youth a simple honest lad could not tell a lie. His answer enraged Pedanius. He ordered him to be flogged with fifty stripes, to be administered by the youth's lover, a slave like him. Again, Prefect Pedanius was quite within his rights. When the youth emerged from Pedanius' chamber, in the firm grip of Pedanius' bodyguards, he called out to his lover who had been pacing up and down outside the chamber, telling him of his sentence. The murderer, seeing that the Guards had left Pedanius unprotected, raged in and beat the City Prefect to death.

Ancient Roman custom requires that every slave residing in the same house as a man murdered by his slave, shall be crucified. There were four hundred men, women and child slaves of all ages, under this particular roof.

The senate-house was besieged by a great mob of plebeians demanding clemency for the innocent. Gaius Cassius Longinus, in a speech stated that 'the four hundred slaves had not protected their master and it would be weakness not to comply with the wise laws of our forefathers'. Senatorial families have long feared slave revolts. A few other senators regretted the necessity to condemn the whole four hundred, not just for mercy's

---

[51] The Romans only considered evidence from slaves bona fide if gained under torture

sake, but as a waste of resources. The Emperor, on my Master's advice stayed clear of the senate, thus securing his popularity with the mob, he also appeased them by vetoing a motion introduced by Cinius Verro, that the freed slaves under Pedanius' roof should suffer deportation.[52] It was still necessary to call out the army to secure the success of the execution and the safety of the senators. It is a curious fact, that the same mob has shown its disapproval in the amphitheatre when Nero allows a hapless victim to live, often a slave. Nero never enjoys cruelty as a spectacle, preferring buffoonery to bloodshed in the arena. On this occasion our master wisely prevailed upon Nero to distance himself from the senate.

On the day of the crucifixion of the household slaves of Pedanius, a public holiday was declared that all might witness it. A good number of our household preferred to avoid the crowds and stay at home, on the advice of our Master who considers these spectacles a bad influence on morals and best avoided.

Later that day, I received a message from our Master asking me to collect Planets and meet him in the Royal Palace. He took us to see Acte; she had been delivered of a baby boy. She lay on her couch with her maids in attendance. After our salutations she told us,

"I have taken the baby to Nero who is happy to accept him as his son, although his mother is only an ex slave and concubine. I am worried that if he lives he will become a threat to Nero or his successor, who will have him killed, as Nero killed Britannicus. Accordingly, I shall always try to keep him away from public appearances and not present him as Nero's son and keep him free from the

---

[52] A large proportion of the plebeians of Rome, were ether freed slaves or sons of freed slaves

clutches of the ambitious, who will use him as a tool to gain power. This way I might be able to preserve his life." She turned to the Master with an uplifting pleading hand.

"Seneca, you have been a good friend and advisor, if either Nero or I should die, will you protect the Emperor's son?" Seneca replied with a weary smile.

"Willingly if I can, but grey hairs are already upon me and my life is in the hands of Nero, who is listening more often to the unsound advice of those who would delight at my demise. I think it unlikely that the fates will allow me to outlive you."

"Just so, that is the reply I expected," she turned to Planets and myself "would you both take on this burden?" I was rather taken aback, being childless, unmarried and not much younger than the Master. I could only proclaim my unsuitability. She told me she did not expect any of us to do it alone but if the need arose, would they secrete the child away in a country villa and give him the best upbringing, away from the corrupting court. "Planets," she continued, "you are young and unimportant in the affairs of Rome, you will outlive us all. Fortuna has favoured you, all I ask is that if any of the present company is able to shelter him from the perils ahead, please do so!"

We all vowed to do our best and Seneca praised her for her wisdom. The swaddled baby was passed around, first to my Master who seemed to know how to handle it, then passed it onto me who didn't and I quickly passed it onto Planets who took it rather sadly and asked where it was injured. Acte asked why she thought it was injured. Planets said,

"Why else would you bandage it up?"

"Everybody swaddles babies, to make their limbs grow straight and it keeps the baby quiet and happy," replied Acte.

"Nobody swaddles babies, where I come from, and we all have straight limbs, we only bandage up wounds" stated Planets emphatically.

"Are you sure?" said Acte. "I don't know of any people who do not swaddle their babies."

The Master fidgeted and butted in ending the debate on swaddling; to my relief,

"Rest assured Acte we shall all endeavour to ensure the survival and prosperity of your child. Come on now, I think we should go and find out what is happening in the city."

Acte rose with the help of her maids and kissed us all in turn as we left.

Business kept me from hearing Planets' story for a time, but at the first opportunity, we took up our usual positions.

"You were going for a morning walk," I prompted.

"Was I? Just when I was comfortable too, oh yes," she said, "in the story, I passed the racks of smoked fish and hanging nets, and walked up the track-way just to see what was there, I heard voices and the squeak of heavily laden oxcarts. Then two mounted soldiers came into view, they saw me before I could hide. So, I ran back to the ship as fast as I could, all the time expecting to hear the sound of galloping hooves behind me and feel the thud of a spear in my back. Once close to the harbour I chanced a look back, there was no one there, I slackened my pace entered the roundhouse and announced my discovery.

"Good," they said, "that will be the tin, how low is the tide?"

It was an hour to low water; the crew went out to make sure the ship lay over on its side facing us, as the tide drained out.

Olondus and the Captain greeted the tin merchant who had ridden ahead of the convoy; they went into the roundhouse with a ewer of wine. I watched the slow progress of the oxcarts lumbering down to the harbour, accompanied by their drivers and six mounted soldiers, two at the front and four at the back. They lined the carts up along the foreshore axle deep in the water, unyoked the oxen and led them off to graze. When the ship had come to rest on the harbour bed with its side facing the carts, the tin merchant called a soldier over and instructed him to round up the drivers to help unload the barrels of beef, using the same method as when they were loaded, rolling the barrels along two parallel poles lashed together about three feet apart. The tin merchant had also purchased some of the iron blooms and had them taken off as well. To my surprise, they did not load the tin onto the ship. The rest of the day was spent eating, drinking and laying around catching up on all news since the last visit.

During the night, I was awakened by the crew rousing up and leaving the roundhouse. I followed to see what they were up to; the harbour was in full flood, the carts half submerged, they released the ship's bow rope and pulled the stern into the shore. As the tide flowed out the ship just had enough water to turn around, it being high enough in the water to clear the banks. This is why they had left it unladen. I returned to my comfy bed and left them to it. The next day at low tide, the round tin ingots were carried in their baskets and stowed in the ship; there were also some pigs of lead. They are very heavy; the men teased me saying that if I carried one to the ship, I could have it to buy my freedom; to humour them I made an attempt.

While the other side of the ship's hull lay exposed, two of the crew scraped it clean, a task already completed for the other side. We were to have the next day for rest and leave at high tide early on the following morning. More of the blackberry porridge was made, it was allowed to cool and cut into slices. This we would eat on the long voyage south, when the seas are too rough to cook. All was made ready for our departure, when a soldier rode in and approached the tin merchant. He had a spare pony with him, they were both in a sweat and been hard ridden.

A pirate ship of the Silures had been seen rounding Ocrinivn promontory.[53] It would likely lay in wait in one of the side creeks and sail down on us after we reached the open sea, where no one could come to our aid and then sail their prize back to Isca.[54] These pirate ships, I had explained to me, are light and fast, being made of wicker covered with hide. They have a crew of seventeen, six-oarsman a side, and one steersman, it also had a sail. It would be impossible to outrun it, or to slip past it in the dark, as the moon would be full at high tide and they would be watching closely. The Captain, Olondus and the tin merchant huddled together in discussion, and then called a meeting of all present. The Captain spoke to all, in this vein,

"We have every reason to suspect that a Silures pirate ship lays waiting to pounce on us, with only six men on the ship our doom is certain. They will have at least three times that number, we cannot delay, the next tide is the spring tide and gives us our only chance of having enough

---

[53] Ocrinivm Promontory: the Lizard
[54] The Silures: a tribe of North Wales Isca: Caerleon on Usk Where there is a hill fort above the river

draft to clear the bottom; or otherwise we will be stuck here until the next sailing season, as soon the winter storms will be upon us. We need good fighting men who are not afeard of the cowardly Silures, the sort of men who are eager to carry home the trophies of war and with my stratagem, their ship as well."

A soldier stepped forward,

"Will there be any extra pay?"

"Double pay!" said the tin merchant.

All the soldiers stepped forward and thudded the ground with the butt of their spears in approval. The messenger soldier pointed out that he, the other soldiers and the ships crew were only eleven warriors against at least seventeen pirates.

The Captain continued, "You are forgetting Olondus and myself, I will fight to protect my ship, Olondus to save his cargo and you Dvmnonii to continue your ancient trade. Are there five more amongst you who are valiant enough to share our glory? If you lack resolve, stay here and guard the oxen."

The tin merchant said that he had agreed to take the ponies to the bay west of the Fal to pick up the men with their trophies.

"That is so my lads, now who is for a boat trip." The Captain looked around slowly; no one moved, the Captain looked around again. An elderly toothless driver with bandy legs stepped forward,

"I have no desire to suffer the pains of old age and to die in my bed, let me be the first to draw blood!" Then another spoke up,

"I have longed for a chance to show my worth in battle, but only this morning I stumbled on a tree root and hurt my back and I don't want to get in the way of the fighting." They all looked at him doubtfully.

"Good" said the Captain drawing the elderly volunteer over to the soldiers. "With this brave man, we shall prevail". He dismissed the others and addressed the volunteers, "Men, these Silures pirates are expecting to attack a weak and defenceless merchant ship, let them continue to think so. When we approach the lower reaches where they may observe us, our main force must hide beneath matting covering the cargo and under the fore and aft decks. When we defend against the first onslaught, a party of four of the nimblest will take the tender and row around to the other side of their ship, board it and attack them in the rear slashing at their exposed ham strings. To assist boarding these men will need to provide themselves with a staff with a spur at the end, for hooking over the gunwale to pull them selves up with. We shall give them a nasty surprise and take their ship; they won't be troubling us again. Now go and prepare yourselves eat well and rest, we sail at high tide, two hours before dawn tomorrow"

Planets told me that she felt frightened, because some of the soldiers were frightened, when she realised they were not afraid of the Silures but of the sea and the ship, she reassured them as an experienced mariner might, and then felt better herself. The elderly volunteer had cut a staff twice as tall as himself he had sharpened it to a point by burning it in the fire and removed the bark at the pointed end. Planets asked him why it was so long.

"So I can be the first to draw blood", he chuckled "Now all it wants is some grease." He put it down and lifted me up face to face between his two outstretched hands; he was stronger than he looked.

"Do you want to live as long as me little girl?" he asked with a gummy mouth, I nodded. "I've never been in a sea battle, but I don't suppose it's much different from defending a palisade on a hill fort. First, they will be hurling stones at us with slingshots, so keep your head safe under something. When they storm the palisade, the ship's side I mean, stay clear of the action! Always keep alert!"

He put me down and I felt he might think it rude or unlucky if I wiped his spit off. So I said, "Thank you, I'll remember that! But why the grease?"

"Keep an eye on me," he said, pointing first to his eye and then to his chest.

The Captain organised and rehearsed all the combatants in their duties for the coming battle. Despite the Captain's advice, everyone was too tense to sleep well that night. At high tide, the ship slipped its moorings and moved about a half a mile down stream, until there was enough draft for all the company to embark. All through the narrow parts of the stream, the tender rowed ahead tethered to the ship and tugged the bow around the bends to keep the ship in the deepest water. All we could hear was the sound of the oars of the tender and the water lapping the side of the ship. Only the small foresail was raised. As the sky lightened, the river widened: we entered deeper water. All the soldiers hid under the mats, the tender was stowed and the mainsail hoisted. The Captain was at the steering oar, the crew kept a sharp look out, one atop of the mast. We could see the open sea ahead; there was a creek on the east bank. The lookout whispered,

"There she is!" and slid down the mast. The whisper went around.

"Not too quiet lads," said the Captain to the crew "try to look normal!"

One of the crew affected a laugh.

"Perhaps, you had better not", said the Captain.

The pirates had seen us. They had hoisted full sail and were rowing after us.

"Make out, you've just seen them, put out the tender and tow the ship as if you mean it! They'll think we are trying to get away! It will make them over confident, remember, as they approach draw along the side opposite to them, ready to take on our boarding party." instructed the Captain.

I was standing on the iron blooms looking astern past the Captains' feet; he was standing on the poop deck, manning the steering oar. They were closing in on us; I looked up at the Captain who was watching the closing pirate ship intently. Rap! A stone had bounced off the water and hit the ships planking. Rap! Rap! Another and another; there were two slingers in the bow of the pirate ship. After slinging his stone, the first man ducked behind the second to reload, who in turn slung his stone. As the gap between us closed, the stones were hitting higher up the hull, until one skimmed across the deck and flashed past my nose, causing the Captain to jump and me to duck under the deck. Olondus pointed and told me to stay there as he did not want his goods damaged. He had taken refuge behind the cargo, with his sword fastened over his back so as not to impede his boarding activity, I supposed. Three more stones passed over our heads, the forth hit the steering oar causing the Captain abandon it jumping down in front of me.

"Keep still men, remember what we practised and wait for the command, it won't be long now" he ordered, in a low confident voice.

I peeked out over the gunwale; the pirate ship had come up fast, it had drawn its nose level with mine, when they suddenly shipped oars, laying them across their ship between the thole-pins and loosed their sail. With their smaller draft and greater momentum, they drew level with us. Then the grappling hooks came over our gunwale and locked tight, our crew pretended to try to cut the ropes and quickly retired when threatened with stone and javelin. With the two ships now locked together, the pirates made their attempt to board what they thought was our undefended ship. As they started to climb over our gunwale the soldiers on command threw off their matting covers; the surprised foe stood over them in a wavering line along atop of the gunwale, unbalanced. The soldiers, protecting their heads with their shields closed together, thrust their stabbing swords upward, eagerly jabbing into the groin and thighs of the assailants.

Olondus had slipped over the side with a soldier to join the two crewmen in the tender. From my position, I could see that the aged volunteer had climbed onto the foredeck lance in hand. Standing with one foot solid on the deck and the other on the gunwale, he lifted his lance and whacked a pirate a vicious blow on side of his head beneath the helmet; he disappeared from view as he collapsed into the bottom of his ship. He was immediately replaced by another pirate who ducked under the attempted blow and grabbed the lance. The old volunteer jerked it back and thrust it forward into the pirate's neck, the grease having prevented the attempted grip. I received a quick toothless grin and I think a wink, before he resumed his work with relish, whacking and prodding where he could.

Olondus' party arrived to the rear of the pirates. That side of their ship was higher out of the water, as the pirates were crowded on the opposite side, attacking us. Olondus and the two crewmen lost no time; using the climbing aids they made earlier they scrambled over the side and commenced slashing at the pirates unprotected legs, like reapers at harvest. The ones that were still standing were obliged to turn to defend themselves. This was the moment when the Captain led the soldiers over and boarded the pirate ship. The slaughter of the pirates was complete, none were spared; their right hands were severed for trophies and tied together by the thumbs later to decorate the soldier's saddles. Exultant were we the victors, cheering as we tossed the dead and wounded foe into the dark sea, the bigger the splash, the bigger the cheer. All fears of the sea banished, the Dvmnonii soldiers took possession of the pirate ship and following the instructions of the Captain, sailed the captured ship into the bay where on the sandy beach their horses were waiting. Our Captain set a course to the south and the coast slowly disappeared. That was the last I saw of Britain, although, there was a fair amount of British blood to be cleaned up."

Chapter 4
Queen Boudicca's rebellion; Ninth Legion disaster.

I noted this part of her story in detail, as my Master, Nero and others had financial investments in Britain and Rome has always a big requirement for metals. It is therefore important that Rome should make this trade secure. The previous Governor of Britain, Quintus Veranius had taken action against the Silures, but only raids of reprisal. His untimely death caused the cessation of these, and of his ultimate plan to subdue the west coast from the south.

Catus Decianus[55] was confined to Rome, while Rome was awaiting news of the rebellion from Britain. It soon came, fortunately the rebellion only occurred in the east, the southern tribes under the Atrebates had stayed loyal, as Planets and Nero had predicted. This was a different version of the rebellion, than that given by Catus Decianus. It was decided to send a strong Imperial delegation to Britain to investigate. It was to be led by Polyclitus a freedman of Nero. He is an excellent choice having no loyalties to any of the Senatorial families and could represent the Emperor's authority reliably and without prejudice. His retinue is to be escorted by a substantial guard provided by Burrus.

My Master, who was instrumental in organising the delegation with Polyclitus, asked me tentatively but knowingly, 'if I knew a person familiar with Britain; a person who spoke the language; a trusted person who could infiltrate and acquire information from the lower

---

[55] Catus Decianus: The ex provincial procurator of Britain, you may remember

orders of British society. Someone like Planets would be ideal; if of course she could be spared?' As a slave she would have no choice if the Master ordered her and he certainly did not require my permission. However, that is not the Master's way but, as he said, 'she was the best candidate'. I thought, the only candidate. If she agreed to do this service for Rome, as a reward he would offer her manumission.[56] I replied that, although only working for me for a year, she would be a great loss, but reluctantly I would ask her.

She agreed to accompany Polyclitus as his scribe's assistant. Planets was concerned that, if freed on her return, she would no longer be needed here in the office as her post would be filled by another. I assured her that the only difference would be that, she would receive a wage for her work and would be free to leave if she so wished, but I hope she would stay. Reassured, she said with a smile,

"Good, it will also reduce the chances of being crucified if one of the scribes goes mad and can't take your scolding"

The Master informed me later, that he had his colleague Burros especially designate a centurion to be diligent in ensuring her safety. As not only was she a valued member of his household, she also had an important secret role within the delegation and was favoured and known to the Emperor. Within six weeks of asking she was back in Britain.

Missives from Polyclitus: We had a rendezvous with the new Provincial Procurator, Gaius Julius Alpinus Classicianus,[57] as arranged at Boulogne;[58] all had had a

---

[56] Releasing the hand: freedom
[57] He was half Gaul He had command of Gaulish Troops
[58] Portus Itius

calm crossing to Dover.[59] There was no evidence of disturbance at Canterbury,[60] nor any where else on route, until we approached the Themes at London.[61] There, the flames of revolt had left the smell of charred flesh and burnt timber on the air, warning us of the catastrophe. However, along the strand were a few ships moored and burnt-out warehouses being rebuilt. Merchants were returning to count their losses. From them I gleaned the information that Suetonious Paulinus had marched here to Londinium,[62] arriving before the avenging tribesmen. Seeing it un-walled he refused to defend it. To make matters worse he allowed his soldiers to loot all the wealth and provisions of the town as though it was defended by the enemy! Those of us with water transport gathered up their families and the meagre possessions and food saved from Paulinus' Army into their ships and made their escape across the river, hiding up in the small creeks of the south bank, until, as they said, the waves of destruction had past.

Planets found a small orphaned boy who had survived the slaughtering attentions of the tribesmen as they believed there was no honour in it, and it offended the Gods. The boy told how the Romans had killed all the animals they did not confiscate for their own use, and threw them up onto a great fire made from timber taken from the buildings, and how all the stores of grain were thrown into the river. Boudicca and the tribesman were incensed by this, as they were short of food and frustrated by the Romans refusal to stay and fight.

---

[59] Portus Duris
[60] Durovernum Cantiacorum
[61] Tamesis at Londinium
[62] Suetonious Paulinus, the governor of Britain

Leaving Londinium we travelled North following the devastation caused principally by the Romans[63] and secondly by the rebels until we came to Verulamium.[64] Here the survivors told the same story. They had only scorn for the Legions saying, "What is the point of us paying our taxes to the Emperor? If, when we need his legions to protect us, they come and ravage our homes, steal our food and run away to hide in their forts, leaving us to face Queen Boudicca! Who is now to protect us from the bands of outlaws roaming the land? Not the Romans, these bands are largely made up of retired or runaway soldiers, and the Legionnaires won't attack their own!"

I agreed with Classicianus that he should transfer as many Gaulish troops as possible from Gaul to the province of Britain, as the trust in the occupying Legions had been compromised. In addition, we agreed to tax concessions for three years to relieve the burden on the afflicted. These arrangements we hoped would pacify the area and allow for the future development and Romanisation, otherwise all might be lost.

Suetonious Paulinus refused to move south to meet us, obliging us to march to his northern base at Lindum.[65] On arrival we discovered that he had left the day before to inspect the frontier posts. I ordered his return; he knew we were coming; that is a job for his staff officers. On his return he was not pleased. He said that, he had not in the past taken orders from effeminate Greeks and neither he or his men were going to start now, and had no intention of answering the questions of a social subordinate. My guards covered the door and stepped closer to my side;

---

[63] The Romans are using a scorched earth policy Having the capacity to supply themselves from other sources
[64] Verulamium: Saint Albans
[65] Lindum: Lincoln

hands clasped weapons. I read to him the letter of authorisation and made it clear that when he addressed me, he addressed the Emperor. Guards bared their swords and moved close to him anticipating the order for arrest. After a long pause, he fell onto one knee raised his right hand in supplication, claiming ignorance of our authority and begging forgiveness. I confined him to his quarters and placed the legionary fortress under the temporary control of the senior officer of the Imperial guard throughout the course of the investigation. I questioned him on the following day, in the hope that the truth would be closer to the facts without the opportunity for his senior offices to confer with him.

Suetonious Paulinus stated that at the time of the rebellion he was in the North West dealing with the wild tribes of the Mona Ins.[66] It was important to subdue these people, as the island is the Druidic focus of the tribes that cause us the most trouble. Here they practised human sacrifice and magic to bring down ruin upon Rome and her allies. On hearing of the rebellion, and having slaughtered the island population and destroyed the groves and temples he returned to the south east at the head of his cavalry as quickly as possible. The main body of Infantry following, they proceeded to Londinium with the cavalry arriving in advance of the rebels. His stratagem was to withdraw northwards destroying anything of value to the rebels and finally to bring them to battle after reuniting with the army. He could thus concentrate his Legions marching from the north with the Second Augusta whom he had ordered from the west. This corresponds with what we found in Londinium.

---

[66] Anglesey

The field of battle was chosen west of Durocobriuis [67] with hills behind to stop the numerically superior rebel cavalry from encircling, this way he was able to protect his rear, the Romans being numerically inferior. The Ninth Legion commanded by Quintus Petilius Cerialis Caesius Rufus had been massacred by the victorious Britons when attempting to prevent their march to Londinium. The Fourteenth Legion with the detachments of the Twentieth and their auxiliaries amounting to nearly ten thousand men was all that could be mustered. The Second Augusta being spread out along a line of forts covering the western boundaries of Roman influence. They were unlikely to have had enough time to form up and march to Durocobriuis. The wisdom of leaving the west unprotected was doubtful. Suetonious Paulinus accused the Second Augusta of cowardice and Poenius Postumus their commander, stabbed himself to death, rather than allowing this accusation to fall on his troops. However, Suetonious Paulinus had achieved a notable victory.

Information from the lower orders indicates that Paulinus was headstrong, capable but never popular. He had a tendency to underestimate the enemy and had been lucky at Durocobriuis in that Boudicca was not present to lead her army into the last battle and that many of her best warriors had been depleted in the battle with the Ninth Legion leaving a large proportion of women in their ranks. I instructed Paulinus to continue border defence, maintain discipline and to curtail expansion until further orders, as his rivalry with Corbulo[68] may incline him to rashness.

---

[67] Dunstable, Bedfordshire
[68] Corbulo has achieved fame fighting in the Eastern provinces and is considered Rome's best general

Travelling to Norwich[69] through the lands of the Iceni, it was difficult to buy food, as the people would flee at the sight of us, evidence of their poor treatment by the Romans. We had to resort to leaving out money to gain their confidence.

At Icenorum I let it be known that I was not there to repress the Iceni, but to establish the cause of the rebellion, on behalf of the Emperor. That if a rebel chief came to me confessing and explaining their action, I would grant a pardon. To the first one I not only granted the pardon, I also returned his estate. Soon the remnants of the Iceni aristocracy were telling me their story: King Prasutagus had acquired an over fondness for Roman wine, encouraged by Catus Decianus who received gifts of the best estates in return for a copious supply. Catus Decianus, with the aid of the Ninth Legion would evict the owners and tenants and sell off the estates to Romans. The starving disenfranchised farmers were then re-employed as slave labour. Furthermore, this foolish King while sampling the delights of Bacchus[70] promised half his Kingdom to Rome on his death. Bacchus assisted by Catus Decianus caused the Kings death. Soon after Paulinus' moved to attack Mona Ins, Decianus summoned to him Boudicca and the chief aristocratic families. Showing them the King's will, he demanded that they all hand over their estates to his Roman agents. Queen Boudicca refused, she said that the King, her husband, had no authority to dispose of property, as under Iceni laws all property is owned by the Queen and passed on through her daughters. Furthermore, she demanded that the property given away by the King illegally should be returned.

---

[69] Venta Icenorum Iceni: local tribe
[70] Bacchus god of wine

Catus Decianus stated that this land was now under Roman law, Boudicca refused to acquiesce saying that the Romans were there by invitation. Catus Decianus had surrounded and packed the assembly with Legionnaires of the Ninth. Losing the argument he ordered Boudicca to be stripped and flogged, one legionnaire held her long hair, while the other flailed her naked torso.

When this work was over Catus kicked the legs away of the semi conscious Queen, and with the same triumphal boot pinning her lacerated body to the ground; tore off the golden torc from around the Royal neck. Raising it above his head he told the Iceni, that from now on they would obey the might of Rome. Now he would fulfil a promise made to the King to find suitable husbands for the two Princesses. He next turned to the sneering soldiers.

"Which of you worthy citizens would like the pleasure of these two fine young ladies, strip them off let the men see what they're getting!"

There was no shortage of volunteers who formed a queue, or encouragement from the rest of the soldiers. Boudicca was forced to watch her two daughters being repeatedly raped before the assembly who, although they could close their eyes, could not close their ears to the screams of the Princesses, Boudicca remained silent. Threatening to do the same to the rest of the Iceni if they dared to defy the Emperor and the might of Rome! He ordered them to leave their torcs and all the gold they had with them and go and do as they were told."

All this information was confirmed by Planets from the lower orders. Rufus the commander of the Ninth Legion along with Catus Decianus had acted towards the Iceni as if they were defeated in war, rather than valued allies. Torcs represent the path of Solis across the sky, the terminals are its rising and setting and the gold is the incorruptible light. Only the highest ranking priests drawn from the pinnacle of society wear them. To place one above your head signifies that you have raised yourself above all other men, effectively claiming Emperorship and to do so without the secret knowledge of the rites, will bring disaster. It is obvious why the ninth legion was obliterated. A husband for one of the Princesses had previously been arranged from the Royal house of the Trinovantes, they were to have succeeded Boudicca. The missives of Polyclitus continue.

We stayed in the lands of the Iceni and Trinovantes, settling the many land disputes caused by the rapacious Catus Decianus, and moved on to Camulodunum,[71] in the land of the Catuvellauni. Here a fine new temple was being raised to the honour of the deified Claudius, by the veterans of the new colonia. All building work ceased when attacked by the Catuvellauni who aligned themselves with the rebels, hearing of the treatment dealt to them. They also had their own grievances with the Romans, as the veterans had displaced them from their own land and exacted high taxes and enslaved them for building labour. They feared the new temple being built dedicated to the deified Claudius would expunge their gods, as he seemed to be destroying their tribe. The veterans overwhelmed by the concerted attack from the three tribes, made a desperate last stand at the new temple. Claudius offered no assistance.[72]

From our other sources we acquired this description of Boudicca. She was a tall powerful woman, with long

---

[71] Camulodunum: Colchester the Trinovantes are between the Iceni to the North and the Catuvellauni to the south

[72] A temple dedicated to the deified Emperor Claudius, the remains can be viewed at Colchester [72] Camulodunum: Colchester the Trinovantes are between the Iceni to the North and the Catuvellauni to the south

[72] A temple dedicated to the deified Emperor Claudius, the remains

brown flowing hair, a penetrating look, and a beguiling smile. She was driven in her two horse chariot, standing tall, by her lover, whom she had chosen from the choicest of her warriors. After her ill treatment she always led her armies and fought with her hair plaited and tied into a knot displaying the scars on her naked back to the warriors behind her. This way she travelled around the three kingdoms displaying her injuries with her two Princesses, rallying the countryside to her cause and killing all Romans they could find, eventually destroying the colony at Camulodunum.

False information lured the Ninth Legion from their fortress, expecting an easy victory they were unprepared to receive the might of the Three Kingdoms bent on the annihilation of everything Roman. The tribesmen cared nothing for their own safety only to satisfy their bloodlust and avenge their redoubtable leader. They successfully turned the Roman flank and massacred the legion from all sides. Losses were high, Boudicca herself receiving many wounds, but to her sorrow she was unable to find the perfidious Catus Decianus, who had run away with all the gold he could carry and escaped to Gaul. Boudicca led her army onto Londinium in the hope of catching him, after learning of his escape she died of her wounds. With her as Leader they would have defeated Suetonious Paulinus and thrown us out of Britain.

I shall continue my work of repatriating the aristocracies with their land, working with Classicianus the Provincial Procurator, to re-establish Romanisation of the Three Kingdoms. It would be advantageous to replace Suetonious Paulinus with a more sensitive Governor at a suitable time. The Imperial Guard, I shall send back to Rome. A detachment of Classicianus' Gauls will act as guards.

The wealth of Britain lies with its ability to produce grain, the most productive part of the province is the south and east. It is paramount that these lands in the east return to agriculture as soon as possible, not only to supply the army in a future expansion to the north, but it could also supply the army on the Rhine using water borne transport.

Verriculla (Planets) is most useful as an interpreter and supplier of information and I apologise to Seneca for not returning her with the Imperial Guard, as her work here is invaluable.

Sad tidings from Rome: news that directly affects my Master and future of the Empire. Burrus died a week before the detachment of the Imperial Guard returned from Britain. He had long suffered from a tumour growing in his throat which eventually caused suffocation. Nero had sent his own physicians to attend Burrus without success. Previously they had successfully saved Nero's life with the assistance of Acte's nursing, she directed the snow cooled baths to reduce his fever and administer the medicine and balms. Burrus together with Seneca had been the palliative to Nero's youth. Now older, his ear started to turn away from my Master's wisdom fixing on the honeyed discourses of the sycophants.

Tiggellinus,[73] by accusing others of having lampooned Nero's performance on the stage acquired the position of senator. He also arranged or Nero to perform in the arena as Hercules with a specially trained toothless lion.[74]

The lion moved around the periphery of the ring, stalked by the Emperor making dramatic gestures as if he

---

[73] Tiggellinus Gaius Ofonius 15-69ad
[74] The first labour of Hercules was to bring Eurystheus the skin of the Nemean Lion that was terrorising Nema Its pelt was impenetrable to weapons, so Hercules throttled it and skinned it with its own claws

was about to jump on its back and strangle the poor thing, when they both became concealed between screens, Nero cried out as if wrestling with the beast. He then emerged dressed in a lion skin and wielding a club. Nero loved the adulation of the crowd and never considered it a debasement of his dignity. On this occasion he allowed them to insist, with the encouragement of well placed soldiers in the crowd, to give a long monologue on the labours of Hercules and rewarded them with showers of coins.

Tiggellinus, to the misfortune of Rome, was made the new joint commander of the Praetorian Guard with Faenius Rufus. (My Master knew Tiggellinus from the time he was a young man working in the house of Agrippina.) With Burrus' support he had succeeded in blocking his advancement until now, although, he did persuade the Emperor to appoint Rufus with him, to counter Tiggellinus' excesses. Rufus was popular in Rome, having attained a reputation for honesty when managing the grain dole, but popularity is no counter to the unscrupulous.

This Tiggellinus had a fine horse stud in Apulia, providing the best race horses for the circus; it was here that he trained the lion. Nero when a child loved playing games with his toy chariots, trying different combinations of horses, charioteers and making sure his own tribe won.[75] He sustained this love into adulthood, spending much time with Tiggellinus at the stud, discoursing on the best breeding strategies and watching the progress of the training. If his interest had stopped there all would have been well, but with Tiggellinus' support he entered races. At first it pleased the crowd. However, he always won

---

[75] The population of Rome was divided into tribes designated by colours

even on the occasion he fell from the chariot and was still adjudged the winner; the other charioteers waiting for him. As he always wore the blue, this caused animosity with the other tribes, neither was he popular with the bookmakers.

Aulus Vitellius[76] is another leader in debauchery, who seduces the young Emperor. He spent his boyhood and youth among the young male prostitutes and hermaphrodites at the Emperor Tiberius' villa Jovis, on the isle of Capri. Here, the elderly Tiberius enjoyed all manner of depravity and Vitellius was an eager apprentice, thus ensuring the success of his father's career in public office and his nickname 'Spintria'.[77] His talents secured him positions in the courts of Gaius Caligula and Claudius. Caligula, for his chariot driving, not because he was any good at it, but Caligula enjoyed the obscene gestures he made during the race and his comic asides. Old Claudius marvelled at his skill with dice, always predicting the right numbers. His stories of how he duped old Claudius with sleight of hand, changing the dice to suit the prediction, always amused Nero.

Vitellius discovered that one of the many loves of Nero was a boy called Sporus. Nero had written a poem extolling his beauty and expressing a desire to marry him if he was a girl. With his consent, Vitellius instructed a surgeon to make Sporus into a girl. After surgery he dressed her up as a bride, complete with dowry and flame coloured veil, and gave her away to Nero in a mock wedding ceremony. All carried out quite openly and with no shame, probably the sort of charade that Tiberius enjoyed while hidden away on Capri. However, Nero

---

[76] Later to become Emperor, in the year of the four Emperors 69ad
[77] Sexual invert

paraded her about the streets of Rome dressed up as an Empress, even kissing her passionately, inviting comments from the crowd such as 'It's a pity your father did not marry a lady like that'. Nero enjoyed this joke as much as the crowd; so long as they did not joke about his lyre-playing, he was happy. He inaugurated a lyre-playing contest as part of the games to celebrate his birthday. During the contest Vitellius the president of the games, would make a public display of begging Nero not to leave before joining in the contest. To which, after much persuasion he did. Nero astounded no one by winning, despite the quality of the other contestants. While in office at Rome, Vitellius used to pilfer the offerings from the temples by substituting gold and silver for brass and tin; and worse, arranging for Nero to rape Rubria, a Vestal Virgin. The punishment for Rubria would have been to be buried alive. On this occasion Nero kept quiet and no one dared prosecute, saving Rubria a hideous death, but not a private shame.

There was a modest turn out to greet Polyclitus and the successful British Delegation on their return to Rome; the Guards led the parade, followed by Polyclitus and his staff. Planets was riding behind the scribes who were leading the servants and then the baggage carts, with more Guards bringing up the rear. All the household staff turned out to give her a cheer. She was pleased to be back in Rome and eager to lounge in the baths, to promenade the shops and to buy some new clothes and luxuries not available in the primitive Northern Province.

I understand that our Master's physician, who examines all the new staff when they enter his service, had advised Planets to cover her strongest eye, and in time with the help of Minerva her weak eye would become as strong as the other. The mistress' seamstress had made her some eye patches, but these had worn out while she was in Britain and had been replaced by ones fashioned out of cat skin by the Guards armourer; new ones were ordered. She told how she had entertained the many orphaned and stray children left by the rebellion, by removing her eye patch and rolling her eyes in different directions. In addition, it was a useful ploy in discouraging hopeful suitors both British and Roman.

She had now grown into a woman. If she accepted our Master's offer of manumission; being under the age of thirty she was not entitled to citizenship, leaving her legally, financially, and physically unprotected. I, on the other hand had purchased my freedom on my thirtieth birthday some time ago now and had subsequently acquired citizenship, I have never married, always being content to visit the professional establishments when the fancy took me. Now getting on in years, I have no heirs to leave my fortune to.

Chapter 5
Cinnamus contemplates marriage and consults an astrologer. A delegation of priests arrive from Jerusalem. Seneca retires from Rome.

Should I ask Planets to marry me, she would then be safe under my protection? I put this question to our Master. He said,

"The important issue of her status would not be a problem after manumission if she was married. You both have to be of the same status for her or your children by her, to inherit your estate according to your will and then you and she will have protection in law. It is not uncommon for a man to marry a girl much younger than himself; often though for the benefit of her dowry. Cicero, for instance, married a girl much younger than himself to please her mother, and was perfectly satisfied with her,[78] although he suffered the odd snide remark about her dowry and keeping it in the family. We are supposing though, that Planets wants to marry you; she may refuse your offer preferring a better looking younger man. Ordinarily, she would have no choice if her father disposed of her to you, but as he is unattainable and as I own her, I could make it a condition of her manumission that she marries you. Although, I would much prefer not to gain her animosity by forcing her into an unwanted union; she may prefer to stay a slave in my house, or some other establishment. She could have made an attachment to a more mature person in a different household and beg me to sell her to its owner."

---

[78] Not so he divorced her, suffering fiscal difficulties paying back her dowry, the reason why he married her She was a distant relation

There is no better or a more considerate master than Seneca, his remarks had an element of teasing in them, neither he nor I approve of forced marriages, and in the two years of her absence she might well have looked upon a young buck in the Guard.

In the absence of her father, our Master offered to propose the union to her. Since her return she had been much in demand, telling her stories of how this and that happened, of what frightful scenes she had seen and details of the journey. She soon tired of all this attention and was glad to be back in the quiet of the office and return to her old job, she observed that it was not as busy as when she left. I had to explain about Burros' death and how our Master was losing influence with the Emperor, in consequence we had less to do. I thought her eagerness to return to work a good omen. Scribonia, when questioned, told me that Planets had made no mention of any particular person she was attracted to while she was away; another good omen I thought.

To reduce the risk of rejection I decided to consult an astrologer, to discover the best time for the Master to make the marriage proposition. The inside of his shop contained an assortment of animal skins stuffed with straw and smelling of mildew. After handing over to him more silver denarii than I would like to admit to, he drew a chart with his little finger on a table top covered with fine sand, showing the signs of the zodiac. He was dressed as a Persian, with baggy trousers and a turban, but spoke with an Aramaic accent. He asked me the hour of the lady's nativity. I told him,

"I don't know"

"He doesn't know," he repeated slowly his little finger poised to mark the chart, he asked me, "the day of her nativity." I told him,

"I don't know"

"He doesn't know," he repeated. His little finger drooping,

"The month?" he prompted hopefully, with lifted eye-brows.

"I don't know," I said, "And I don't know the year either, does it matter? Can't you use my details?"

"If there is absolutely no information you can tell me about her, that's the best we can do"

"All I can tell you is that her name is Verriculla; she comes from Britain, has no money, and is boss-eyed"

"And you want to marry her?" he looked puzzled, frowned and slowly shook his head.

"Ah!" He exclaimed raising both hands in the air.

"Her eyes, of course she has the eyes of Venus, all is clear!"[79] I gave him the details of my nativity. After placing seven pebbles on the chart to represent the sun, moon and planets and carefully moving them around to new positions leaving trails in the sand; he confidently told me that in fifteen days time, Venus would be closest to my nativity sign, and on that day a successful proposal is almost guaranteed.

I walked home quickly, and went straight to my Master to inform him of the most propitious day for him to propose the nuptials. Mistress Paullina[80] and my Master were enjoying a meal of figs, and drinking strawberries crushed into milk; when I entered they offered me a seat. After the normal pleasantries I managed to steer the subject of conversation to the astrologer and his recommendations. My Master chided me that it was a complete waste of time. Most of the so called astrologers

---

[79]Venus: goddess of love Romans thought that Venus was cross-eyed Petronius, Satyricon 68

[80] Seneca's second wife

are charlatans ready to take money from the gullible. I protested that everyone consults an astrologer before taking important decisions.

"No, No," he said, "not me, you're too late, I put it to her this morning when you were wasting your time and money on dubious predictions".

"What did she say? Yes or no," I asked a little exasperated.

"Firstly I explained to her that my position at court was becoming more tenuous; there are factions jealous of my influence with the Emperor, who will instigate plots against me. Tiggellinus, to gain evidence, will exercise his right to have all the slaves in my household tortured. I am preparing for this event, but recommend that you accept manumission for this reason alone. Citizenship will not be allowed to you as you are too young, leaving you an unprotected woman. My secretary Cinnamus has instructed me,[81] if I am in agreement, to ask if you will marry him after your manumission. As his wife you will hold a reputable position in society, never wanting for the necessities of life. He has over the years, by exercising frugality, amassed a not small fortune, and he will inherit more from my will when I die. Considering my ill health and the growing power of my enemies, that event won't be long. Cinnamus is rather dull, but he is kind and not given to excesses of vice. And at his age is unlikely to bother you very much in bed; he won't have the stamina for it at his age. Not in the too distant future he is certain make you a young widow: a widow with a nice little nest egg: a widow who is free to do as she likes. I confirmed these rhetorical points with encouraging winks. And I also

---

[81] The first time the writer gives his name

added that I believed Cinnamus must be very fond of you to make this generous offer."

I thanked him for advocating my case so exactly.

"And what was her reply?" I asked again resigned to patience.

"Have some figs dear Cinnamus, they're fresh only picked this morning and some of this goat's milk too with the crushed strawberries, it's very good" Mistress Paullina interjected and instructed the servant to hand me the figs and pour some milk. Our Master continued. "There was none, I told her to think it over in her own time and tell you when she is ready". I tried a sweet fig and a cup of the strawberry milk. The master could not tell from her demeanour the nature of her response. I slowly made my way to the office, not knowing what to do there; I looked around the silent and empty office in the early evening. Seeing the stack of writing tablets piled neatly on the table, I wrote a few lines on the top one:

Fortune favour me,
Bring bright the day
That your pure heart
I long to hear.

Over your sweet tongue
Through the lips ripe for
The softest kisses,
Let your breath say yes!
O yes.

Placing it on top of the stack for her to delete in the morning, I left the office undecided as to whether it was good or bad that she was unable to read. Next morning, when I returned to the office, Planets was deleting the tablets and chatting to the early scribes as they limbered up their fingers. When she turned and noticed me she gave a big smile. Was her smile saying 'Silly old fool I will not marry you, your old flesh disgusts me?' I must let her tell me when she is ready.

Later that morning I was summoned to the Master. He told me that he intended to hand over the bulk of his Estate and wealth to the Emperor, to assuage the jealousy at court.

"Without the wealth generated from your estates, will you be able to throw the lavish dinner parties and receptions your position at court demands?" I asked.

His answer was as expected,

"I shall ask the Emperor for permission to retire to the country, pleading poor health and old age. As you know it's not the first time poor health has preserved my head;[82] and what do I want with such vast wealth? It only attracts intrigues and danger, when real wealth lies in a happy and tranquil life. However, I shall keep a few of my choicest farms and villas about the Empire, don't worry I will not be another Diogenes the Cynic.[83] Now we must draw up a list of assets to be disposed of and slaves deserving manumission all to be done as soon as possible, before the next census.[84] Bring me a list of all my

---

[82] The Emperor Caligula sentenced him to death in 37ad as he was told that Seneca was dying of tuberculosis, he revoked it Seneca's ill health may have come to his rescue in 41ad when Claudius sentenced him to death He suffered from asthma all his life; the smog of the City would have exacerbated the condition

[83] Diogenes practised a philosophy of absolute independence of people and worldly goods Seneca in his writings is much influenced by the Cynics, leading to the charge of hypocrite, by Saint Augustine and others

[84] Disposing of property before the census saves paying tax One method of manumission is achieved by the expunging of the slaves name from the list of property of the owner, given at the census

possessions and we can go through it to see what is to be kept."

I returned to the office to supervise the drawing up of the list. These days I dictate to my scribes, it saves straining my eyes as my sight is not so good at close work, so I only use it sparingly. Planets was there as always, standing by ready to help with any chore, her presence distracted me: I had a strong disconcerting desire to move close and stroke her blond hair, feel her soft pale cheek blushed with red, and savour the sweet odour of her neck. Not the behaviour I would tolerate in the office, and certainly not the behaviour becoming of the senior secretary. I asked her to fetch a pitcher of fresh water, while I regained my composure. On her return she poured out a cup of water for me and placed it on my desk. Odd behaviour, why had she not handed me the cup? I walked from the opposite end of the office, to my desk where I had been supervising the removal of the scrolls I needed from their pigeon holes. Lying there, wax side down, was a writing tablet. Unusual, I picked it up turned it over and read:

Yes, But I have so little to offer.
Except, that by Fortuna's favour
She will share, when my life
My body is in your care.

All had gone silent; everyone's eyes were focused on me. I looked at Planets and she looked at the floor, sheepishly.

"Go on then!" someone said.

Then Planets ran over to me and we embraced. I held her close, my left hand on her head, as I buried my nose in her hair and I thought I saw money change hands between two of the staff.

"Did you compose this verse yourself?" I asked.

"Not only did I compose it, I wrote it as well. I've been practising all the time I was away with the help of friends and I can read too!" she said proudly. "Next I shall learn to take shorthand so you can dictate to me, if you are willing"

She was now nearly as tall as me and looked straight into my eyes. She had agreed to the marriage and revealed talents beyond the expected. Truly Fortuna's favour was on me that day. I held her head between both hands feeling her soft, silky blond hair between my fingers and kissed her as tenderly as my excitement would allow; more money passed hands.

"Come on now!" I said in a stern voice, smiling "We have a lot of work to do!" There was a lot of work to do and it took a good time before completion. The Master came to see me with another problem.

"Tiggellinus has foisted a delegation of Jewish priests on to me to look after. It might be prudent for peace and tranquillity to keep them away from your school friend Paul as they all seem very argumentative; perhaps he would like to visit our villa in the country to see his converts out of town".

The story of these priests is amusing. Their most holy temple of Jerusalem built by Herod the Great with the help of Roman Engineers and money, has its holiest sanctum on the top of a levelled hill. They believe that their God, whose name it is forbidden to utter, resides there, and that is the only temple where he accepts sacrificial offerings. Our governor Festus[85] has constructed a room and platform for King Agrippa's own entertainment and pleasure above the highest wall. It has views all over the city, including the most holy sanctum of the Temple, where he can witness the sacrifices. The high priests were scandalized! How could their God live amongst them? And how could they sacrifice when exposed to the profane gaze of the un-circumcised? When Festus' duty caused him to leave Jerusalem, these priests surreptitiously had the intervening wall raised, blocking Festus's view. When Festus returned he demanded that the wall be lowered. This they said was impossible, as it was built by the hand of God. Festus, doubting the veracity of their account of the miraculous masonry rounded up the local masons, who quickly admitted without much torture, that they had raised the wall. The priests countered that their hands were guided by God and only God had instructed them. With the aid of a bit more torture, the masons revealed that the priests had told them to build up the wall. Again the priests countered that God was speaking directly through them; as a revelation of the divine would be too much for the un-initiated. It was therefore decided that the issue should be arbitrated in Rome.

Festus' report stated that the whole country is full of faction and dissent. His predecessor Felix[86] had to protect the lower order of priests from the higher order, who set their men to steal their food causing them to starve. The Jews send gold tribute to the Temple from all over the

---

[85] Porcius Festus had also sent St Paul to Rome under guard for his own safety That is why Seneca did not want them to meet, Paul being in the pay of the Romans

[86] Marcus Antonius Felix 1-60ad: a freed Greek slave of Antonia, Claudius' mother He rose to become procurator of Judea And sat in judgment of Paul, he refused to release him for his own safety Acts 23, 24

Empire; it is kept in strong rooms within the court of the male Israelites. It is therefore, essential, for security to know what and who is going in and coming out of the temple, particularly the court of men; the holy sanctum is also within the court of men. Festus said that while he was away dealing with a particularly nasty band of robbers, who the Jews call the Sicae,[87] on account of the shape of their daggers. Daggers that they use in a cowardly way, for if a prominent man boldly spoke out against them or refused them money; they would send one of their kind to kill him, by stabbing him in the back when he was amongst the multitude attending a festival. These Sicae had banded together under a leader, who claimed to be the rightful king of Judea, and preached that the uncircumcised should be slain; particularly the hated Romans. In Festus absence, the inner wall had been raised deliberately to prevent the observation of the temple from the Antonia fortress, built high on the orders of Herod the Great, precisely so that the treasure and the High Priests could be guarded in an unobtrusive manner. The temple is rectangular with the Antonia fortress at the north end, overlooking the outer wall, with Agrippa's new room built above the royal portico in the south, so he could watch his priests whom he had appointed, performing the sacrifices and rituals.

The ten priests arrived in Rome and crossed our threshold, headed by Ismael the high priest and Helcies the keeper of the treasure.[88] They were not popular with the staff. They refused to eat unless the food was prepared and cooked under their own supervision, our cook and kitchen staff considered this a gross insult. They allowed

---

[87] Sicae: a dagger in the shape of a Roman sickle
[88] The King appointed high priests from the sons of former high priests of different families, one of the causes of contention at Jerusalem

no contact with the female staff, as they said they are impure. Our entire tableware was rejected, as it was not made of gold. Nero was not interested in them and sent them off to see Poppaea Sabina.[89] Poppaea allowed them to retain the wall at its present height. Festus had requested that Ismael and Helcies be retained in Rome to prevent more disruption. Poppaea agreed to house the two priests at her villa as religious practices are of interest to her; we packed the rest off back to Judea with haste.

The Master and I spent two days discussing the list of properties to be disposed of, and of the slaves deserving manumission prior to handover to Nero.[90] The following two days we spent compiling and amending the list of properties omitting the names of the slaves due to be freed, and a special list for the Vindicta ceremony,[91] with Verriculla's name at the top. On the fifth day the Master and myself, with my future wife Verriculla and two other slaves from our household, who were to be freed, dressed in our best clothes with the Master looking resplendent in a new toga; we filed down to the court for the Vindicta ceremony. The Master by his rank, held precedence over other speakers. After observing the protocol of the court, he read out the list for manumission. There were no objections and he declared before the court that these people were not his property. Verriculla and the other two slaves were given a copper tablet stating that they are not owned by Seneca and are free men. The other freedmen who could not attend the ceremony had theirs sent to them. Our party returned home to celebrate with a special meal. I took advantage of the occasion to announce the

---

[89] First mention of Poppaea: Nero's future wife
[90] The freed slave will have obligations to Seneca if he releases him before handover
[91] To declare in law

date of our wedding in six days time, that day being propitious, as no disasters had befallen on it; on the seventh we leave Rome.

Nero, who had always been fond of our Master, was reluctant to allow him to retire. The master pleaded his age, ill health and flattered Nero that he was now capable of governing on his own, without the aid of his old tutor. My Master told me that Nero's body was becoming bloated with excesses of food and wine and his reason was relentlessly degrading under the weight of fear, shame and unrestricted power. Despite the adulation and wishes for a long reign that are heaped upon him, Nero knows his end won't be peaceful and suffers from nightmares of how Gaius was murdered at the theatre and of Claudius's poisoning by Agrippina.[92] These fears are exploited by Tiggellinus who brings spurious evidence of plots before Nero in order to eliminate his own enemies and confiscate their property. Nero, always short of money for his schemes accepted his old tutor's gift,[93] thereby giving his permission to leave Rome and retire to the country.

---

[92] Agrippina: Claudius' wife and Nero's mother
[93] Cinnamus' Master Seneca had become Nero's tutor at Agrippina's request, shortly before he became Emperor A tutor was more than a teacher of rhetoric and philosophy; he was a moral guide and a source of wisdom

Chapter 6
The wedding. Seneca in peril.
The move to Nomentum.

The morning of the wedding I spent relaxing at the baths. Normally I don't attend until the afternoon when business is over. Today, being special, I arrived an hour before noon. I try to maintain a good pace walking up the Capitoline Hill to Agrippa's Baths close by the Pantheon.[94] The effort is worth the sweat and I consider it part of my warming up exercises. I joined in a game of catch with some of the other early bird customers and suffered their good natured ribald remarks, comparing my fumbling performance with the leather ball, to my likely performance at my coming nuptials. Those of us who felt sufficiently invigorated moved onto the divesting room, where we stripped off and left our clothes with the attendant.

These baths here in Rome are naturally the biggest and grandest in the Empire, the entire interior is faced with marble and it was on a marble slab in the tepidarium,[95] that I had my body oiled and scraped clean of dirt with the strigil.[96] To look my best for my bride on our wedding night, I also had the slave remove all my body hair; he used the hot wax method; I believe his previous job was an interrogator of prisoners. My Master maintains that sweating should occur only through

---

[94] Agrippa: supporter of Octavian and helped him to become Emperor Augustus He married Augustus' daughter Julia Their daughter Agrippina and Germanicus sired Future Emperor Gaius (Caligula) and Nero's mother, Agrippina Augustus made him responsible for many building projects in Rome including the Pantheon and baths

[95] Tepidarium: a warm and usually the biggest room

[96] The body was cleaned by first oiling the skin and then scraping off with a curved blade called a strigil

exercise and not from sitting in the caldarium,[97] so I just stayed in there long enough to acquire a moderate sweat, before plunging into the frigidarium.[98] Then partaking of the baths as fancy took me, finishing up with a good swim and returning to the tepidarium, to relax and chat to acquaintances, whilst enjoying a gentle massage. The baths have pleasant gardens, with fountains to moisten and clean the air of the pervading wood smoke and stench that emanate from the thousands of cooking stoves here in Rome. As usual I finished off my visit with a stroll around these gardens. While enjoying the scent of the roses, an acquaintance of mine, who works in Tiggellinus' household, came to me with a warning that a man called Romanus had clandestinely denounced my Master Seneca and Calpurnius Piso[99] for plotting against Nero.[100]

I returned home with a quicker pace than my usual downhill saunter, immediately to report this disturbing news and more than a little excited at the imminent proceedings of the afternoon. The Master smiled and said,

"Don't worry, dear Cinnamus, I have seen off better men than Romanus, today we have more pleasurable duties to see to; don't you think?"

I took a light meal of bread, cheese and a glass of wine to steady my nerves before the ceremony. Acte found me and chided me for being nervous at my age.

"That's why I am nervous" I replied as she grabbed my arm and marched us off to join the gathering of

---

[97] Caldarium: the hottest room, nearest to the fire The English word cauldron comes from the Latin caldarius: warming
[98] Frigidarium: coolest room and pool
[99] Gaius Calpurnius Piso: A popular, rich, courteous man, an excellent speaker This accusation was to have disastrous consequences later
[100] It is impossible to know from the text whether this man is a paid spy, or a concerned friend, however it does highlight Cinnamus' anxiety about security in the first letter

witnesses, friends and staff, waiting in the central courtyard. In came the Master and Mistress Paullina, with Planets behind supported by Scribonia, who had arranged Planets' hair in the traditional way with six locks piled on her head and covered with the flammeum.[101] Her white flannel tunic was tied at the waist with the traditional brides knot and around her neck, hung a garland of periwinkle and mint.[102] I hesitated because she looked so beautiful; both her blue eyes were steadily fixed on me, in a soft smile. I marvelled she had no eye patch.

The Master, who was acting as Planets' father, beckoned me to approach and I formally requested that Planets be given as my bride. He agreed and I passed over to him the token coin.[103] Paullina brought forward Planets and taking our hands joined them together, my right in her left. We now stood together. For Juno to bless the marriage,[104] a pig was offered for sacrifice by the Auspex,[105] who ordered the cook to prepare it for the celebrations on the following day. The Master read out the marriage contract; Planets or I should say Verriculla, was joined to me as my wife and I was to provide her with hearth, home, protection and instruction in shorthand. In return Verriculla gave me herself, her youth, charm and beauty of soul, along with her other talents; enough for any sensible man. It was signed by the five witnesses. We stood close together all this time, our bodies touching, hands still folded together as Paullina had placed them, but behind us now. We led the way into the refectory, thigh brushing against thigh. As we parted to our

---

[101] An oblong flame coloured veil
[102] Periwinkle: Vinca, the Latin name means to bind The Romans used mint as an herbal medicine and perfume
[103] A residual tradition of bride-purchase from archaic times
[104] Juno: Goddess of marriage
[105] Auspex: the priest and best man

respective seats, I caught the perfume of her hair and felt her warmth drift away.

Verriculla sat next to Paullina and I next to the Auspex. I noticed the cook had provided plenty of rocket and no lettuce,[106] obviously cook was of the opinion that I needed all the help I could get. At end of the meal, the Auspex announced it was time to claim my bride. She traditionally clung to Paullina protesting and I had to go and drag her away, finally capturing her in my arms. This pantomime is accompanied by shouts of encouragement and advice by the audience, according to their sex and how much wine they had drunk, culminating with a cheer and the stamping of feet. The whole party moved off to the rear exit to parade around to the front door, symbolising the traditional moving of the proceedings to the groom's house, where the bride, my bride, would now live. It was headed by three boys, the centre one carrying a wooden torch bearing the brides fire to her new home. Normally, the groom has to hurry on ahead to greet the procession on its arrival at the groom's house, I simply walked through the villa and past the Larium[107] in the hall and opened the front door.[108]

Most brides carry a spindle and distaff, symbolising her role as a wife; Verriculla chose more appropriately a stylus and writing tablet. As they approached, I heard the clatter of the walnut shells as they were thrown on to the ground and stamped upon. They demanded entry for the new wife on arrival. I accepted the gift of the bride's fire

---

[106] Eruca sativa: Rocket, according to Pliny an aphrodisiac Lactuca sativa: Lettuce had the opposite effect This feast in the bride's house is provided by the groom

[107] A shrine usually close to the front door dedicated to the household deities, the Lares

[108] The proceedings here are imitating families who normally live in separate households

from the torch, and lit the house lamps before carefully discarding it.[109] Next the bride rubbed the doorway with beeswax and ink, in lieu of the usual fat, oil and wool, representing a more domestic role. I successfully lifted her across the threshold without touching the doorway or stumbling, ensuring our continuing good luck. The Auspex placed a bowl of water and a lamp before Planets; she first had to place one hand in the water and then brush it across the flame of the lamp, the elements of life. A choir of the best singers of the household gathered around the nuptial spirit bed, for the singing of the epithalamia.[110] Then the guests lined the route to the nuptial chamber door, Paullina led my lovely bride to the singing of the choir, between the two rows of wedding guests and into the nuptial chamber.[111] When Paullina emerged from the chamber, the singing turned into a cheer and died into silence; all faces turned to me.

"Cinnamus, your bride is ready and waiting for you," she announced followed by another cheer. I felt excitement, tinged with apprehension as I acknowledged the good wishes of the guests as I passed between them to the door.

Verriculla sat on the bed; her golden hair had been loosened and brushed over her left shoulder, the garland removed. Over the bed suspended from the ceiling were hanging vines of grapes, around the room sprays of white

---

[109] Romans were superstitious about this torch and how it was extinguished and disposed of If placed under the bed for instance the marriage will end prematurely

[110] Epithalamia: wedding songs, to encourage consummation A miniature nuptial bed was set up and decorated outside the marriage chamber for the use of the couple's connubial lares or sprites

[111] Paullina has been acting as a Pronuba: a once married matron with a living husband She would advise the bride, pray and offer sacrifice with her, and prepare her for her husband

lilies,[112] each one reflecting the pure light of its own lamp burning the first pressed olive-oil. Rose petals had been scattered on the floor.[113] Verriculla stood up; we moved together meeting mouth to mouth, in a kiss so tender that my vision blurred, and the scent of roses drifted up from the floor. I felt the need to say something. I sat on the bed trying to draw her down to sit next to me; she avoided my intention but sat across my thighs with her arms around my neck; I held her with one arm around her back and the other across her legs, hugging her to me.

"I do love you wife", I whispered close to her ear adding, "I hope you can love me being past my prime and you so young."

But she interrupted me with a kiss and whispered in my ear,

"I love you too husband, I always have and always will, not because you purchased me, took me in and taught me the ways of the office, you had no choice, Fortuna decreed it. Not only because you are gentle, sober and educated, shunning the blood hungry masses at the arena. I love you because you're you, and I always intended that I should be yours; and I knew I would be from the time that we first went to your chamber and you looked at me lying on your bed. Now I rather hope you are good at untying knots, Paullina tied this one particularly tightly, with the words,

'This will keep him busy for a while.' " [114]

She stood up and presented the sash of her tunic for untying, I bent forward to see closely how it was tied, she

---

[112] Lilium candidium : Madonna lily, a sacred flower of Juno Fruit was present to represent fertility and for refreshment

[113] Cleopatra is said to have seduced Mark Anthony, wallowing knee deep in rose petals

[114] Paullina acting as the Pronuba Had tied a special traditional knot Her role is to heighten passions to ensure the bride conceives

stroked my head, and I wished my eyes were better seeing close to, and my hand steadier. I untied the knot and dropped the sash and looked up into her eyes and she looked directly into mine.

"You have beautiful blue eyes," I told her "will you still use the patch? Let me kiss those lucky eyes" I stood up gently kissed both lids.

"The doctor told me when I first came here that if covered the good eye the other would grow in vigour to match it, and it has! I intended two good eyes for you, as a present on our marriage day, I can give you so little else." As she said this, she knelt on the floor removing my slippers and caressing my feet and slid her hand up my calf as she stood up.

"The knot's undone don't be shy," she said with her back to me and her arms in the air. With both hands I slowly raised the hem of her skirt revealing her slim legs widening to her hips and slightly parting beneath her firm round buttocks, her narrow waist and a perfect muscular back; I could not resist kissing the nape of her neck and nibbling her ear before freeing her entirely of her dress.

"Don't move; your skin is exquisite in the lamp light." Its shadows revealed the enchanting contours of her lean flawless back.

"Can I turn round now? You must not touch; Paullina has prepared a special game"

"Slowly with your arms raised" I replied. I dropped to my knees,

"Tell Paullina I can't help myself."

I placed my hands on each buttock and pulling her to me I caressed her warm soft belly with my cheek, there I hoped new life would spring.

"Come let me undress you and I will tell you of Paullina's game."

I stood up and allowed her to remove my clothes.

"Paullina has," she kissed me as she spoke, "anointed me." And she spoke slowly apparently admiring each part of my body as it was revealed "with six different kinds of perfume."

She named them between kisses: "There's Southern Wood, Saffron, Hyssop, Lavender, Rose and Violets. In the morning Paullina will ask you what secret places she has hidden them, she said to remind you that violets are dedicated to Venus."

Verriculla pulled aside the bed covers and laid down, stretched out an arm towards me, her lovely body too, had had its hair removed. I went to her and gently kissing her...[115]

I awoke to a shaft of daylight, shining through the crack in the shutter straight on to my beloved's radiant face and glinting off her golden hair. Blue veins showed through pale translucent skin, whiter than Parian marble[116] from the hair-line on her forehead down to her breast topped with the raspberry red of her virgin nipple. Trying not to wake her I slipped on some clothes to pay a visit to the latrine. On the way back I stopped to offer a prayer at the shrine. I prayed that if Verriculla had conceived a child; let it not be the cause of her death as so often happens. Rather than that, she should not conceive at all as such a loss would be unbearable. Verriculla had crept up behind me startling me by pulling my left ear and dodging round to my right.

"What are you praying for?" she enquired.

"For the future and good fortune"

---

[115] The original text is contaminated here preventing further translation

[116] Marble from Paros is renowned for its whiteness

"You don't want to worry about that, I think I owe Priapus[117] my gratitude."

We returned to bed to consume the remainder of our fruit, Verriculla reaching up to pull of a grape and dropped it into the bed and pulled the covers over us.

"Good dog, go and find it," she commanded, wriggling deeper into the bed. I dived down nose first, sliding the tip my tongue along the length of her body in and out of her navel. I was searching between her legs, when, in walked Paullina and coughed, Verriculla tugged the bed clothes over my exposed upper legs.

Paullina, between giggles said, "In my capacity as the Pronuba, I have to enquire if the marriage is consummated"

The giggles turned into laughter. Verriculla was laughing as I struggled to resume a more normal position in bed keeping discreetly covered. Emerging into the daylight I noticed Verriculla's face, from her head down had turned as pink as a rose. I lifted the cover to see how far down my love this delightful hue had travelled; she pulled it down tight with her arms.

Paullina continued, "Cinnamus, if you have been performing that way round all night, there is no hope of consummation"

We all enjoyed a good laugh!

"And I see the Southern Wood[118] I placed under the pillow is still working!" She nodded to the bulge in the bed covers. It was my turn to blush, just a little!

---

[117] Priapus: the god of sexuality and fertility, the son of Dionysus and Aphrodite, the gods of wine and love He had a notable phallus; donkeys were sacrificed to him

[118] Southern Wood under the pillow was thought to heighten the passion

"Well, have you consummated? How many times? Now tell me, both of you, by raising the correct number of fingers when I say now-now!"

Our fingers did not correspond we all looked at each other, laughter resounded as Paullina left us, with a wave of her hand!

Mid-day we joined our friends for the banquet that rounded off our wedding. The Master kept to his diet of plain food and fruit, abstaining from the wine, although it was from his own estates in the south and considered to be the best in Rome. We all enjoyed the pig sacrificed to honour Juno the previous day; cook had roasted it in honey and then served it with a honey and mulberry sauce. The Master provided acrobats, jugglers and dancers accompanied by flute players, for our entertainment. He was prevailed upon to read us his comedy, the Apocolocyntosis of the Divine Claudius, especially written for the amusement of the young Nero; these days Nero is not so easily amused.[119] He finished with a speech of valediction to the staff that would be staying on in this house with the new master; that is whoever Nero awards it to.

"As you know, I must restrict my wealth so that ill-fortune's weapons miss their mark. Let us learn therefore, to increase our self restraint; to curb luxury, to moderate ambition, to soften anger with restraint; to regard poverty without prejudice and to practice frugality; even if others are ashamed of it, to curb as if in fetters unbridled hopes and a mind obsessed with the future. It is not possible that all the manifold and unfair desires of life can be so repelled. Although, many a storm will not assail those

---

[119] Seneca pokes fun at the deified Claudius' reception, on meeting the other gods

who spread their sails ambitiously, but to be wise is to run for a port. Even in our studies where expenditure of time is proved most worthwhile, justification depends on moderation. What is the point of the huge libraries that their owners cannot read? Better to devote yourself to a few authors, than to get lost among many. Some people collect racks of scrolls, not for the scholarship and wisdom coiled within but for the decoration of their dining rooms. How can you excuse a man who collects scroll cases of citron-wood and ivory, amasses the works of unknown or third rate authors and then sits yawning, admiring the appearance of his volumes and their labels? We are tied to fortune, some by a loose and golden chain and others by a tight iron one. Does it matter how we are chained, when we are all chained in the same captivity, and those who chained us, are they not also bound? Some are chained by high office, others by servitude. Think your way through your difficulties by justice, kindness and generosity; prepare defences against disasters. Let us banish ostentation and measure things by their qualities of function rather than display. Let food simply banish hunger and drink banish thirst and adjust your style of dress to your way of living rather than the latest fashion. Envy not those above you for the higher their pinnacle the further their fall.[120] When your friends are separated from you remember; Nomentum is only four hours walk from Rome,[121] making a day visit to meet your friends and family possible".

Our old friend Paul of Tarsus stood up and blessed us, with one hand on each of our heads in the name of Jesus the Nazarene, the founder of his sect. He said that

---

[120] Compare Seneca's dialogue on Tranquillity of Mind
[121] Seneca's villa at Nomentum is 14 miles from Rome Seneca's humanity to his staff, not so common in Roman society

the Jerusalem Church are outraged by his intercourse with the uncircumcised and even brother Peter here in Rome would not approve of blessing the uninitiated. He considers that his two gods are for all people.

After his speech, the Master spoke intimately to both Verriculla and myself, in the following vein.

"Although I have spoken to Nero and turned the accusation against myself and Piso by Romanus against Romanus himself, Piso remains fearful but refuses to appease Nero by ceding to him some of his wealth. This may be the cause of my premature demise, which cannot be that far off, in consideration of my health and age. I intend to spend the interim in travel and composing letters and dialogues for those who may deem them useful, now or in the future. You might use your wide knowledge of the Empire and its communications to supply works of literature by myself and other authors to the men of the Empire. A business that would benefit the world: wherever Roman feet tread. I shall bequeath an appropriate property to you and fiscal resources for this enterprise, if you are agreeable that is. But it is not necessary to wait for my death, you could commence on our arrival at Nomentum."

Verriculla was so pleased at this proposal; she embraced a surprised Seneca, and said,

"We might find a customer in far away Britain!"

All the scrolls and the Master's letters had to be packed into their boxes, ready for transport to Nomentum, with some of the office equipment and furniture. The number of scribes was reduced to three, with Verriculla and myself. Most of the furniture stayed behind with the household goods, as Nomentum is fully equipped. The Master sent us on ahead with the office furniture and a team of slaves, to set up the scroll racks and guard us on our journey. I already knew the resident staff and greeted them with varying degrees of pleasure, proudly introducing my new wife 'Verriculla'. Gossip travels fast; they already knew of our marriage, but were surprised to discover her organising the office and our new quarters, before hurrying back the next day to supervise the transport of the precious library of our Master Seneca. She had in a short time understood the collected value of the minds of the great philosophers and writers, including our Master, who intended to spend his retirement in assisting his friends and the rest of the world, with his philosophy. It is true that Verriculla has been lucky, but it's only through the tenacity of her character she has achieved abilities in reading and writing in Latin. Her ambition for knowledge frees her from the greed, jealousy and spite, which often afflict us; it gives her confidence to organise the slaves.

Now while I am waiting, I have time to describe the Master's villa here at Nomentum. The front entrance is approached through a portico of eight columns with rooms on either side; the door opens into the well proportioned hall, with a larium in its niche beside the door. There is a passageway on the right to allow a concealed access to the kitchen garden, and on the left are the doors to the kitchen and storerooms. Straight on there is a pleasant courtyard with two semi circular colonnades, this will be a fine place to sit in bad weather as the overhanging roof gives protection. Opposite, is the cheerful inner hall, the walls are painted with a frieze of hunting scenes, red borders on gold panelled background. The dining room beyond is paved with a fine geometric mosaic, there is also a half round mosaic in the apse at the far end of the room. The mosaic in the main part of the room forms a rectangle between the couches; side tables are placed around the room.

To the left of the courtyard are three bedrooms, one of which is ours. It is a room of fine proportions, twice as long as it is wide; it has two doors, one to the outside. The bed is at the far end, with a wall panel above it bearing a peacock painted in green and red tones, standing amongst foliage. Opposite the bed are a small table and two chairs, also two comfortable wicker chairs with lamp stands beside them. Along the walls are our chests for clothes and personal affects; that is, when they arrive. Further along, to the left of the dining room are three more bedrooms and a gymnasium, with access onto the courtyard.

To the right of the inner hall is the bath suite with the heated swimming pool and exercise area. It is doubtful whether the Master will heat the swimming pool; preferring the austerity of a cold dip! There are bedrooms above this for the staff and next to this, to the right of the courtyard, are the library and our scriptorium. Here on the library wall between the racks of scrolls is a small mosaic of Socrates nobly drinking hemlock. A terrace walk communicates

Open Garden with view from Private Apartment

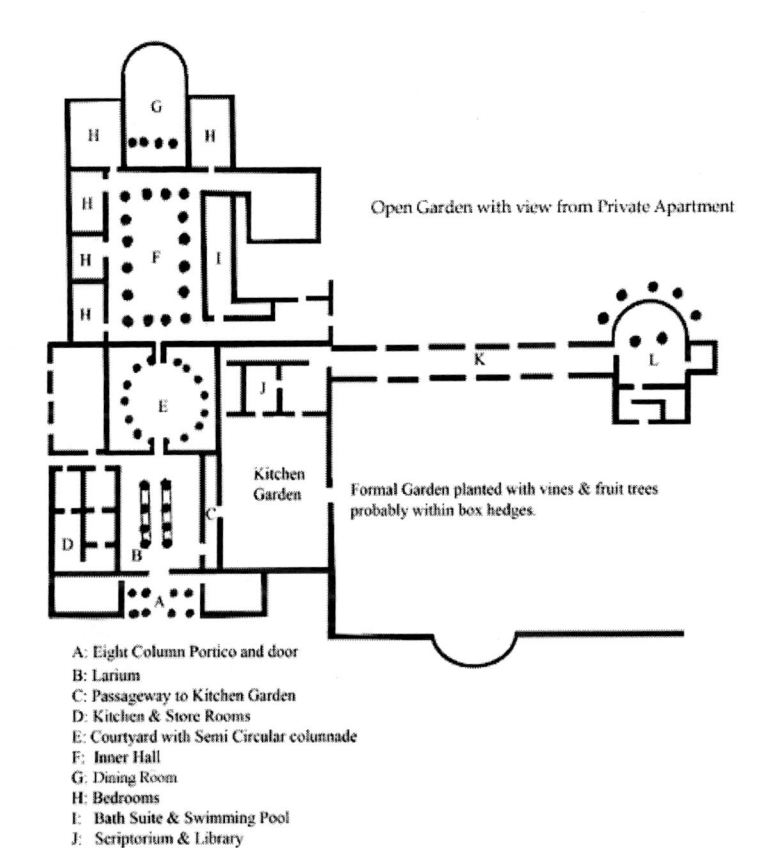

Kitchen Garden

Formal Garden planted with vines & fruit trees probably within box hedges.

A: Eight Column Portico and door
B: Larium
C: Passageway to Kitchen Garden
D: Kitchen & Store Rooms
E: Courtyard with Semi Circular columnade
F: Inner Hall
G: Dining Room
H: Bedrooms
I: Bath Suite & Swimming Pool
J: Scriptorium & Library
K: Walkway
L: Masters Private Suite

through the garden to the Master's private suite. His study is provided with folding doors opening onto the garden, and in the winter the bedroom is heated by its own hypocaust.[122] This is a quiet place away from the household staff, ideal for personal writing and study.

The garden is laid out with a vine pagoda, grafted espalier apple trees, box hedges, flowers and herbs. There is a smaller dining room with a view onto the garden behind the rooms to the right of the front entrance. Unlike Rome, no separate dining room is provided for the staff in this villa, as the Master thinks it is no disgrace to eat with the staff in the small dining room. The villa is comfortable although austere, as it lacks the opulence fashionable today with the new rich.

The master is encouraging us to supply copies of his and other works for sale. We are looking for agents, shopkeepers or private persons, who wish to purchase copies of literary works. If you know of such a person in your city let me know. We are repeating this request to all the Praefectura[123] in the Empire, to promote business and the fame of our master.

It is now a long time past noon, I was expecting them four or five hours ago. I hope they are all safe and our possessions too, especially the strong box with all my savings! To relieve my growing anxiety, I will dispatch a messenger on a swift pony to find out what has happened to them.

The messenger has returned with the news that Nero had announced his intention of divorcing Octavia and raising Poppaea as Empress. Scandalized, the protesting people of Rome had blocked the streets preventing access to the gates. At last I can sleep in the knowledge that all are safe.

---

[122] Hypocaust: hot air and smoke is drawn through cavities under the floor and out through cavities in the wall, to heat the room

[123] Praefectura: office of a prefect, the governor of a town or district

Chapter 7
Faenius Rufus and others fall to Tiggellinus. Nero divorces Octavia. How Britannicus and Agrippina died. Nero marries Poppaea.

I can now give you a full account of the incidents prior and subsequent to the one that effected our move. Tiggellinus by insidious suggestion had convinced Nero that his colleague and co-Praetorian Guard commander Faenius Rufus, had in the past an illicit friendship with Nero's mother Agrippina. Rufus' honesty and reputation for fair dealing had gained him the approbation of the populace, thus his removal caused the first stirring of their censure. Also, Nero had feared the last two members of the Julian line: Rubellius Plautus and Faustus Sulla Felix and to keep them away from the centre of power, Plautus had been exiled to Asia and Sulla to Gaul.

"The name of Sulla has excited the Gauls. Although he pretends to be lazy, he is biding his time to end his poverty in exile at the head of an armed insurrection. How can we suppress sedition so far away?" Tiggellinus' insinuating words aroused an unjustified response with Nero. Five days later assassins smashed their way into the innocent Sulla's house in Massilia.[124] He was at dinner, and between courses they cut his head off. When it was presented to Nero as proof of the deed, he considered sadly that it was disfigured by greyness.

Tiggellinus aroused Nero to take action against Plautius,[125] by the opposite stratagem, telling him that,

---

[124] Massilia: now the port of Marseilles
[125] Not the Plautius of the British invasion

"Plautius is rich and active, he resents his enforced retirement in Asia and he plans to escape to join Corbulo, who having mighty armies at his command could set Plautius up as Emperor.[126] Moreover, Asia had already risen to his support." Fictitious stories like this were spread around Rome and were amplified by idle credulity to the point where rumour had it that a party of soldiers sent to arrest Plautius had joined his supposed rebellion. Lucus Antistius Vetus, Plautius' father-in-law, sent an exslave of Plautius to warn him sixty Praetorian Guardsmen were on their way to assassinate him and that he should "grab the nettle" destroy this small force, and rouse up a rebellion, as a bold end is as good as a tame one. No doubt he preferred to see his daughter as Empress, rather than a widow. But Plautius had a loyal heart and refused such advice, preferring an imperturbable expectation of death rather than a hazardous anxious life. The killers found him stripped for his midday exercise, supervised by the eunuch Pelago who was Nero's watch-dog. Pelago's slaves had reported that no attempt had been made to communicate with Corbulo. The guards, nevertheless, acting on orders, removed his head. It was taken to Nero, who, on seeing it, announced with a sigh.

"How could such a long nosed man have frightened me so?"

Nero ashamed of the fear that caused him to murder Sulla and Plautius was unable to admit to their death in the Senate, but feebly asked only for their expulsion as agitators, as if they were still alive. On these grounds the senate voted a thanksgiving for the Emperor's safety and the expulsion of the two murdered men, although innocent. This sycophancy by the Senate caused greater

---

[126] Corbulo, had armies in Syria defending the Eastern Empire See note 42

disgust than the crimes of the Emperor who concluded that his misdeeds were accounted meritorious. Thus encouraged, Nero proclaimed his divorce from Octavia for barrenness and announced his intention of marrying Poppaea.

The plebeians demonstrated their feelings against Nero's action, without the fear shown by the Senate, their crowding of the streets in protest had prevented our move from Rome. The following weeks Nero divorced Octavia, after she had received the ominous gift of Burrus' old villa and the recently murdered Plautius' estates. Poppaea lost no time in becoming Empress, her first action was to secretly bribe one of Octavia's household staff to accuse her of adultery with her Alexandrian flute player. Tiggellinus had this flute player and the rest of her household questioned in the usual way. Some of the maids were induced by pain to make false accusations, but most maintained their mistress' innocence. One brave slave, a woman, retorted gallantly to the leading questions put to her between lashes.

"The lying mouth of Tiggellinus is fouler than any part of her pure mistress Octavia." How different from the noble members of the Senate! This information was gleaned from our informer in Tiggellinus' staff: the one who tipped me off some time ago about Romanus.

Octavia was married to Nero when she was thirteen, at the behest of Empress Agrippina, to cement Nero onto the throne over Octavia's brother Britannicus, Claudius' son by his third wife Messallina. Agrippina, after she had successfully persuaded Claudius to adopt Nero as his heir, poisoned Claudius with mushrooms and set her own seventeen year old son Nero on the throne. From the first, she tried to dominate and rule through Nero as his mother and empress; in time Nero began to resent his mother's interference. She was considered a great beauty and all though all his life Nero had loved strong women. It is said she tried to regain her position by making him her lover, a ploy that she had always used successfully; rumours of their incestuous relationship became the talk of Rome. In her own history she denies this, claiming that her relationship was nothing more than the usual affection between mother and son, and blames Octavia for spreading the wicked gossip. She used every opportunity to decry Octavia in Nero's presence.

The unfortunate Britannicus, four years younger than Nero, could not remember to call him by his new adopted name 'Nero' and annoyed Nero by calling him 'Athenobarbus' his birth name from his father. When Agrippina started showing Britannicus affection, Nero feared that she might treat her son the same way as she had treated her husband, with poison, and supplant him with the young Britannicus whom she could dominate. To forestall this possibility Nero had him poisoned first. He did it while they were dining. A drink first sampled by the taster was offered to Britannicus who found it too hot; the poison was in the liquid used for cooling it. Britannicus went into convulsions before Nero and Octavia. Nero sat back and observed that this often happened to epileptics and that his sight and consciousness would soon return. Agrippina tried to control her features but her evident consternation and terror showed and that like Britannicus' sister Octavia she too, was innocent. Agrippina realised that her last hope of power had gone. Octavia although young as she was, had learnt to hide her sorrow, fear, affection and all the natural feelings. After a short silence, the banquet continued.

Octavia, it is said, had virtually died on her wedding day. Poison had removed her father and her brother. Her mother in law had shown her nothing but animosity; she had previously had her hand in her mother's suicide, having her mother accused of secretly marrying the consort designate, Gaius Silius, in Claudius' absence. Agrippina soon after became Claudius' wife and Empress. Now she, the innocent Octavia, Nero's unhappy wife and Empress, had been successfully ruined by her successor Poppaea. Although the last accusation of infidelity had proved unsuccessful, thanks to the loyalty of her staff, Nero had her banished to Campania under close military surveillance.

The people of Rome when they realised what had happened demanded her return, haranguing Nero at the games and circus, disparaging Poppaea, for they loved Octavia. To placate them he proposed to reinstate Octavia as his wife, the Emperor was acclaimed and worshiped again. Poppaea's statues were overturned and Octavia's were showered with flowers, the crowd setting them once again in the forum and temples. Detachments of guards protected Poppaea from the rioters by clubbing them and forcing them back with the point of the sword.

Always a savage hater, Poppaea was now mad with fear of the mass violence and at Nero's capitulation to it. She fell at Nero's feet haranguing him with the words,

"How can you let these things come to this pass? Am I not your wife, the Empress? Why are you allowing Octavia's slaves and dependents to threaten me? They stir up the people of Rome and commit in peace time outrages prohibited even in times of war! Octavia only has to nod her head in distant Campania and our lives are threatened. What if she found a leader to champion her cause? What have I done wrong? Who have I injured? I, who am going to give an authentic heir to the house of the Caesars."

Poppaea's arguments played on Nero's fears and angers in turn. A new charge had to be brought against Octavia to discredit her in the eyes of the public, and an excuse for her elimination was created. It was decided to concoct a confession of adultery from someone's compliant; someone against whom a charge of revolution could be made believable; the fleet commander at Misenum, 'Anicetus' was designated for the task. He was offered the choice of either, a large amount of money and a quiet retirement away from Rome in Sardinia; or death as an alternative. His rapacious and warped character had no difficulty in preferring to add to the crimes he had already committed for Nero!

Allow me to digress once more, to tell you about the first crime he committed for Nero, and how he gained his position of fleet commander as his reward. You will recall that as Nero wearied of his mother's interference in state business and her maternal chiding, she tried to restore her influence by binding him to her sexually, although she denied it. She was seen passionately kissing him on the mouth and offering her breast for him to kiss and fondle, even before the Empress Octavia.[127] The talk in the taverns was that she wanted to marry her son, just as she had married her uncle Claudius to satisfy her lust for power. To avert Nero from his mother's wiles, Seneca introduced our gracious friend Acte, an ex-slave, a lady about the same age as Agrippina; her equal in beauty, Nero fell passionately in love with her. Agrippina's chagrin was that of the scorned lover and a rejected mother. Nero avoided her company at court and with her ambitions

---

[127] Such behaviour may not be so odd; this family considered themselves neo-deities Agrippina may have been eliciting reverence, as the mother of a god: Nero The cult of the Egyptian mother goddess Isis, was popular in Italy at this time, she may have been emulating her to ensure fecundity

temporarily thwarted; she retired to her country palace at Antium, in a vile temper. She now had become odious to Nero and he sought advice on how to kill her. She understood the perils of poison better than most, and how to protect herself from it: it was she, who understood how Germanicus was poisoned. Assassination by the blade risked the possibility of failure and discovery and the heinous accusation of matricide descending on the Emperor would be considered ill fortuitous to the Empire. All seemed impossible as her staff were devoted to her and beyond bribery. Nero confidentially consulted Anicetus, his previous tutor before our Master, who reminded him of a recent naval spectacle where a ship had been constructed to break apart in a mock battle. If he had command of the fleet at Misenum he would build a similar ship for Agrippina. This ingenious but foolhardy plan found favour with the theatrical notions of the young Emperor, who immediately reconciled himself with his formidable mother, announcing that,

"Parents' tempers must be borne! One must humour their feelings."

All was prepared for the festival of Minerva celebrated at Baiae.[128] Nero met her with open arms and escorted her to Bauli, a palace on the bay between Cape Misenum and the waters of Baiae. Amongst the ships drawn up onto the strand at Bauli one was more sumptuous than the rest. Agrippina had been accustomed to travel in luxury ships manned by the imperial navy, and regarded the new ship as a token of filial love.

The next day Nero invited her to a banquet. He sent a sedan-chair to convey her to Baiae. Burrus was there and our Master Seneca who told me that she was given the seat

---

[128] Celebrated from the 19-23 March

of honour to the right of Nero,[129] the party went on for a long time. Nero was boyish and intimate, making her laugh and then asking her advice on serious matters of state. When she left he saw her off, gazing into her eyes and clinging to her, reluctant to let her go. Anicetus' naval escort conveyed her to the awaiting ship, ready, or so it seemed to her and those not privy to the plot including Burrus and our Master, to row her back to Bauli. Heaven, it seemed was determined to reveal the crime, it was a clear starlit night and the air carried every sound, the sea was placid; perfect conditions for the viewers lining the shore. When the ship was under way and was heading towards Bauli a short distance off shore; large suspended weights were made to drop through the lightly constructed roof of the cabin. Agrippina's couch had been placed beneath those weights; she was reclining on her couch with her lady in waiting, Acerronia, at her feet. They were saved by the high sides of the couch deflecting the weights; her other lady in waiting Crepereius was killed instantly.

Part of the hull had been left weak to break open when struck by the falling weights allowing the ship to sink, not all the crew were informed of the plot, some dived over the side to repair the hole by covering it with a mat, others rushed to one side in order to let the sea water in through the lower oar ports; the ones not privy to the plan going to the opposite side to rebalance the ship. Acerronia became demented, attacking all she could get at, her screams clear to those on shore above the din and the chaotic shouting of orders. Then her screams abruptly ceased. She had been clubbed to death. Although wounded in the shoulder, Agrippina kept her nerve in the

---

[129] This incident takes place in 59ad before Burrus' death

confusion. She lay prostrate as though dead. When the opportunity came she quietly slipped into the rising water and swam away. She was picked up by a fishing boat coming to the rescue, and taken on to her palace at Bauli.

She reflected that her only chance of survival lie in feigning ignorance of the plot. She dispatched a message to her son, stating that by divine mercy and by his lucky star that was shining on her that night, she had miraculously survived a terrible accident at sea, she begged him not to visit her, as she needed peace and quiet to recover. Calmly she ordered the wills of her dead ladies in waiting to be found, and their property sealed. Nero was half dead with fear when he learnt of his mothers escape, he insisted that she might turn up at any moment with an armed band of her devoted slaves or soldiers and incriminate him for the murder of her friends.

Burrus and our Master were awakened. On being informed of the debacle, they feared the risk of civil war should Agrippina flee to Rome and gain the support of the Senate and Legions; they advised Nero to act quickly. Already crowds of people had gathered on the foreshore and some waded out to sea, offering prayers of thanksgiving to Neptune for the delivery of the Emperor's mother, their blessed Agrippina to safety, others thronged her palace day and night with torches lit, awaiting news. In Burrus' opinion it would be impossible to bribe her guard, as they were devoted to the daughter of Germanicus.[130] When the messenger arrived from Agrippina he was escorted to the Emperor. Disbelieving his mother's credulity, and fearing her intention might be

---

[130]Germanicus: Adopted son of Augustus, had success in Germany revenging the defeat of Varus six years earlier, gained popularity with the Army with his dashing style The Emperor Caligula was his son and Agrippina's brother, hence her popularity with the people and army (Germanicus' gains proved transient)

hostile, he drew a sword from the sheath of one of his guards and threw it at the messenger's feet, pretending with feigned indignation that he was an assassin, sent by his Mother. Anicetus announced that he would go forth and avenge this wicked attack on his Emperor, Nero cried out,

"Go quickly and take plenty of good men ready to obey orders. This will be the first day of my true reign; the magnificent gift of an ex-slave."

When no message arrived from her son, Agrippina expected the inevitable, and sent her staff away for their own protection. It was the end that Agrippina had always anticipated; years ago she had consulted an astrologer who predicted that Nero would become Emperor and kill his mother.

"Let him kill me, he will become Emperor" was her fatal reply.

Anicetus dispatched a party to clear away the devoted well-wishers still surrounding Agrippina's palace; ashamed, it is said, that his face should be seen. He entered with two naval officers and found her in her bedroom accompanied by a lone maid, who terrified, fled.

"You have come to enquire after my health. You will inform my son that I am better. No! You are assassins! Then strike here!" She stood up putting her hand to her womb, challenging them to thrust in the points of their gladius;[131] they recoiled from the act; she reclined back onto her bed and looked upon them with contempt. Then, they surrounded her bed, clubbing her to death from behind; striking at the head, as they could not face her.[132]

---

[131] Gladius: a short sword used by Roman infantry
[132] Agrippina died in 59ad aged 44

Thus Anicetus' first crime for Nero, made Nero an orphan; the second was to make him a widower, earning the Emperor's gratitude and a quiet, but luxurious retirement in Sardinia. At the next Council of state Anicetus confessed to allowing Octavia to seduce him, and then attempting to persuade him to command the fleet in a rebellion against the Emperor. Adding to these lies he told them that Octavia had secretly aborted Nero's child; forgetting that the original grounds for divorce by the Emperor was the Empress' barrenness.

Octavia at the age of twenty had led a faultless life, only these lies made up by Poppaea and her faction allowed for the order for her execution to be given. She, hardly a living thing any more, was surrounded by guardsman; she pleaded that she was no longer Nero's wife, but his sister, and of their common ancestors.[133] The order came a few days later. She was bound and all her veins opened. It is said that she was so terrified that the blood did not flow, even after immersing her in a very hot bath, so they resorted to suffocation to finish the job. Her head was cut off and taken to Poppaea, for her to exult over.

Later, Nero had two of his ex-slaves poisoned for not supporting his marriage to Poppaea. Doryphorus was devoted to Octavia and loyalty to her forbade him to recognise the new Empress, preferring to serve Octavia in heaven, than Poppaea on earth. The other ex-slave had grown old and very rich in the Imperial service. Nero thought it immoral for a man to live so long when he was needy of his denarii. How often the loyalty and conduct of slaves is exemplary, unlike their masters.

---

[133] Nero's step sister

Chapter 8
Business in the senate. Poppaea's princess. Cinnamus becomes a father. The cult of Osiris.

I will refrain from telling you about the military situation in the East as you are in a better position to know than I. The senate has passed a decree, that bogus adoptions will not be considered when elections to office or inheritances are considered. This decree, it is hoped, will bring an end to the unedifying practice of the ambitious and greedy, who hastily adopt any available orphan they can lay their hands on, whenever a plum position is in the offing. As to whether the candidate achieved his ambition or not, the adopted son soon finds himself once more an orphan and kicked out into the street. The men who had taken on the responsibility of rearing sons for Rome had complained about how easy it was for the irresponsible childless man to gain office in this way, leaving them with the burden of family and no income. The same applies to inheritance, how often a quick adoption is arranged just to satisfy the terms of a will. Let us hope that these measures result in better management of the Empire.[134]

An example of the worst sort of governor was demonstrated at the trial of Claudius Timarchus, a Cretan native. He had gained enormous wealth and influence by the excessive extortion of taxes. A familiar story you may think, but in his pride he boasted that,

"Nothing could be done on the island without my approval, even if the Provincial assembly wishes to offer their thanks to me the 'Governor' and they often do, they

---
[134] The Lex Poppaea, (9ad) gave preference to family men in regards to promotion and inheritance

must first consult me." This insult to the senate would never have arisen if an honourable man with a good family had been made governor. Thrasea,[135] speaking for the prosecution, cited the laws on rapacity, bribery and corruption and proposed that the defendant be deported from Crete. He went on to make points that will be of interest to you living in the provinces,

"Let us face this unprecedented provincial arrogance, with a measure befitting Roman honour and dignity, without diminishing our protection of individuals. Rome's reputation must be restored to the hands of Romans. Once we used to send praetors, consuls or even private citizens to report on the state of the provinces. Then nations trembled on the verdict of one man! Now we court and flatter foreigners, to hear what they say about a province and its governor, and then they go so far as to expect us to prosecute him! Granting that we should allow provincials some measure of power, we should nevertheless frown on governors wallowing in empty eulogies from the governed. To oblige is often as harmful as to offend, and some virtues provoke hatred. That is why our officials start well and end badly. By prohibiting votes of thanks and popularity hunting, provisional government will be fairer and steadier."

These opinions received a warm approval. As no senatorial decree was before the house on the subject, it could not be carried. Later, however, on the Emperor's instruction, a decree was passed forbidding votes of thanks to governors. We can supply a full transcription of Thrasea's speech, indeed we can supply a copy of his, the 'Life of Cato the Stoic' if you are interested. We employ the

---

[135] Paetus Publius Clodius Thrasea Died in 66ad He tried to preserve the dignity of the Senate Nero prevailed upon the senate to order his suicide, owing to his criticism of the Emperor

most skilful and diligent scribes and only use the best new papyrus for our copies; the sides of which are expertly clipped straight and smoothed off with pumice before tinting them black to prevent fraying. We can roll them onto bone or wooden rollers, whichever you prefer. A red label is attached for easy identification when it has taken its place amongst the others in your library. Then the whole lot is immersed in cedar-oil to prevent the predations of moths and worms.

Verriculla has promised that I shall be a father around the Summer Solstice. All the ladies of the household are excited by the prospect and the younger members of the staff are incredulous that a person of my age could manage such a feat unaided. A certain scribe, who we kept on after the move, I understand, has greatly benefited financially from taking wagers on this happy outcome of our nuptials. It will be a comfort for me to have a child to leave my wealth to.

Nero too, is ecstatic as Poppaea has given birth to a girl at Antium. It was the birthplace of Nero and therefore considered propitious for the nativity. The senate approved the naming of the child Augusta; to discharge its vows it proclaimed that a temple of fertility is to be built and also two golden statues of the fortunes of Antium are to be placed on the throne of Capitoline Jupiter. The whole senate including our Master were obliged to pay their respects and journey to Antium.[136] Except for Thrasea, who was barred by Nero, a bad portent for him, although Thrasea took it calmly. During their absence there was a great storm in Rome, the new gymnasium was struck by lightning and the colossal bronze statue of the Emperor was melted by the hand of Jupiter. The whole of Rome

---

[136] Antium: Anzio, coastal town 35miles south of Rome

considered that it was an ill omen for the Emperor and the dynasty of the Julians. Thrasea said nothing.

It is now six months since Nero's daughter Augusta was born and sadly two months since she died. She has been declared a goddess by the senate and awarded a position on the God's ceremonial couch together with her own shrine and priest. We have to smile at the depths of sycophancy to which the senate has plunged. The Roman Knights have long complained that the Roscian Laws, that allotted them the first fourteen rows of seats at the theatre in front of the people's seats; did not apply to the circus. The senate amended the law to allow this. Horse racing is more popular with the people than the theatre. Knights taking up their newly allotted seats soon found themselves the targets of obnoxious missiles; quite rightly, in my opinion.

Our evenings are occupied by Verriculla's shorthand lessons. I settle down in the comfy chair, she brings the wine over to the small table by my side and pours out two beakers, she then fetches over her writing tablet and settles down across my lap. Thus with an arm around her back and the other holding her thigh I cuddle her up, while she practices her shorthand to my dictation. We make this cosy situation fun by writing silly things. In this pleasant way I discharge my marriage vows, and we hope the baby will absorb a talent for writing, although I don't expect it will be born with the knowledge of shorthand. It is bound to be clever; I hope it is lucky too. Verriculla I notice is getting heavier; her tummy is swelling with new life and her young breasts are taking on the divine form for motherhood. Each night, I anoint her precious, bountiful body with soothing, sweet smelling unguents and pray over it for the safety of both, and then, shower it with the kisses it deserves. Her skin, of pure white, is now the epitome of youthful health and her hair shines with golden vigour. Most people think she is too thin; to an old scribe like me she is quite beautiful, clever and kind. Although, she can be firm when dealing with the merchants; and is always looking for quality at the best prices. Life goes on. Not much happening in Rome as the Emperor is grieving for his daughter at Antium.

The ladies of the household are helping us to prepare for Verriculla's confinement. The midwife is at the ready, Verriculla has stubbornly refused to allow the baby to be swaddled. It caused no little consternation with the Egyptian midwife who thought it vital to the baby's survival, and should be done as soon as it had been presented to the father.[137] The Egyptians are always keen on bandaging. There are people in Rome who follow the cult of Osiris. They believe Osiris taught the Egyptians agriculture and Isis, who is both his sister and wife, benefited the world by the introduction of marriage. You may know the legend, but I will tell you it in any case; as I have only recently learnt it myself from Scribonia, who has joined the cult here. She has become an enthused proselyte, and tells me confidentially of their rites.

Osiris and his sister god Isis and their sibling gods, Seth and Nephthys, are the natural progeny of the sky goddess Nut, and her consul, the Earth god Gab. Osiris had dominion over the land and brought forth the corn and food of the earth. The people worshipped him, and all were happy. This period is celebrated in the early winter, with feasting before Osiris when the temple is decorated with sheaves of wheat saved from the harvest and baskets of fruit and flowers, hymns and canticles of

---

[137] If the father found a defect with the baby he was allowed under Roman law to kill it

praise are offered. Seth grew jealous of the adoration of the people for his brother and tricked the unsuspecting Osiris into getting into a box while he was under the influence of wine. Seth immediately secured a lid and deposited the box into the Nile; it washed up on the seashore of Phoenicia close to Byblos.[138]

This rite is celebrated at the winter solstices; they make an ithyphallic likeness of the god and commence a festival of drinking and music. The priest offers wine to the god. Girls dance before him. Then a priest, the incarnation of Seth the god of the underworld, drags a box before Osiris; the dancers scatter; all turn their faces from the scene. The priest deposits the likeness of the god into the box and sets off to the nearest river, followed by the wailing congregation.

Seth found the body by the sea and chopped it up into small pieces, scattering it over the land of Egypt; except that is, his penis that was unfortunately eaten by a Nile carp. The land is barren.

The next rite is on the night of the next full moon. The two sister goddesses Isis and Nephthys are implored to reincarnate Osiris, in form canticles led by two priestesses. They promise to find the scattered parts of their brother and with the help of Anubis restore Osiris so that spring time fertility is assured.[139] Anubis, when he binds the resurrected body, is charged with replacing his organ of fertility. The congregation leave the temple at day-break. They collect samples of soil from the fields and estates all

---

[138]Byblos: A Phoenician city at the Eastern end of the Mediterranean It had a long history of trade with Egypt particularly exporting the famous cedar wood of Lebanon Archaeological evidence attests to 18th and 19th centuries b.c trade from her port

[139] Anubis: the jackal headed mortuary god Some sources say that he was the son of Nephthys and Osiris, conceived when Osiris accidentally mistook Nephthys for her sister Isis You'd think she would have noticed

over the district and take them to the priest and priestesses.

At springtime they re-congregate at the temple. The priests have concocted an Osiris, out of linen bandages using the soil mixed with corn seed as filler. I am assuming this as Scribonia had not seen it herself; it is done in secret. The entire congregation, led by the priests and priestesses, in turn anoint Osiris with Nile water. They actually use local water, to which a small amount of Nile water is added. Thus the fecund properties of the Nile bathe the burgeoning God. When the seeds have sprouted all come and witness the mystery. Osiris, complete with a splendid phallus and sprouting corn, is paraded around the fields with jubilation. Isis successfully copulates with her resurrected husband and gives birth to Horus. Isis is depicted nursing Horus. Scribonia says that Verriculla should bathe in the purifying sacred Nile waters, before Isis, so that Isis will assure a safe delivery and an abundance of milk.[140] Of course I have to make a payment first and another if the baby lives for more than six weeks. I don't think these exotic deities are any more powerful than our Greek or Roman gods. Although people do, and there are priests of Anubis working in and around Rome today who perform embalming and guarantee a passage into the after-life, they are not short of business. That is all I can tell you, until Scribonia tells me more. Do you know, the rich are having their furniture inlayed with expensive tortoiseshell, nothing new about that you say, but the tortoiseshell is painted to look like wood; Just another example of the foolish conceit that abounds in Rome.

---

[140] Baths for this purpose are shown in small votive statues from the vicinity of the public baths at Tell Atrib Egypt

Verriculla has given birth to a girl, the midwife recorded the exact time of the nativity. Both are healthy and I have received congratulations all round and a certain scribe, I notice, who should be diligently working at his desk, has been sneaking about collecting bets from people.

Baby and mother have survived the first six months, always a critical time. I am relieved that we are living away from the fevers that currently infest Rome. The local people talk incessantly about their next trip to Rome, and about 'Petraites' their gladiatorial hero, and whether Petraites is to be greeted by Charon.[141] I do hope they do not return with the fever, Charon is busy enough.

Nero was not content with performing his songs in his gardens in Rome at the youth games; he went to Neapolis to perform them in public. He thinks that only Greeks have an understanding of artistic merit capable of appreciating his talent: Rome was relieved.[142] The theatre there, a wooden construction, was packed not only with the cream of Neapolitan society and important visitors, but also with ordinary people, and soldiers too. When the performance was over and the theatre empty; it suddenly collapsed. When Nero examined it, he proclaimed that 'fortune' had saved a catastrophe by not allowing the theatre to collapse before his performance, thus preventing the good citizens from enjoying the talents of their Emperor. There were those who took the opposite view, that it was an ill omen, a warning that the Emperor of Rome should not debase himself by appearing on the stage in front of common people, reciting and singing for

---

[141] Charon: the ferryman of Hades, who carries the dead across the river Styx, to the underworld Also at the gladiatorial games it was the name of the attendant who drags the dead from the arena, with the aid of a hook

[142] Neapolis: Naples, founded by the Greeks

entertainment. The gods would not countenance such behaviour, and clearly showed that Nero would fall like the theatre. Encouraged by the reception at Neapolis, he planned to continue on to Greece, but while staying at Beneventum before embarking across the Adriatic, he attended a gladiatorial event paid for by an ex-slave, one Vitinius.

Vitinius had started out working as a shoemaker, it caused him to have a misshapen back, or so he never tired of telling people. With age, he acquired the wit to amuse and his master took him into his household, trusting him evermore with his affairs. Vitinius became rich handling his master's business, not necessarily so his master, but the master was happy. Vitinius purchased his freedom and used his wit to gain lucrative Army contracts supplying leather and leather goods. Naturally, he is despised by the old families who mock his bent back earned in lowly toil. He replies by throwing them money, telling them to buy a new toga or get their old one washed.[143] They don't demean themselves by picking it up, however, the street urchins who have no such qualms, scrabble about in the road, impeding their pompous progress; to the delight of the on-lookers and the irritation of the lictors.

Vitinius's show was popular with the crowd and Nero enjoyed it too, as there was buffoonery alongside the usual gory violent events. Perhaps the affair at Neapolis had frightened Nero, he vacillated at Beneventum,[144] then decided against going to Greece, issuing a decree that he planned to visit the Eastern provinces as he wished to see Egypt, but that although absent, efficient running of the

---

[143] The toga was only worn by born free male citizens, his jibe is against the old land owning aristocracy who despised the new men's wealth

[144] Beneventum: now Benevento, Campania, Southern Italy 50k north east of Naples a town where 6 roads converge

Empire would continue. The Empress Poppaea, I believe, has been long been a devotee of Isis, otherwise why else go to Egypt? Nothing but corn and desert; of course, I know, to buy papyrus. Only the best, for the best composer and emperor will do; don't you think?

Nero, abandoning Egypt returned to Rome. He made offerings to the Capitoline gods for his safe return, then descended down the Capitoline hill carried on his litter. As always acknowledging the Romans standing on steps of the forums lining the Sacred Way; he loves an audience. I have heard this report from more than one witness; that after descending from his litter and upon entering the temple of the Sacred Flame, Vesta caused all his limbs to tremble, the Goddess setting a fear upon him, or agitating the fear already within him more likely. The priests held him steady while a vestal virgin guided the offering hand. Nero made a proclamation that he would stay in Rome, he had looked into the faces of the Romans, and recognised their fear of his absence, and their private lamentations at not being able to gaze upon his countenance.

"Just as in private relationships the nearest are the dearest," he said, "so to me the Romans come first: I will obey their entreaties to stay, and not cruelly deprive them of my presence." I wonder how the deprived the Egyptians felt.

Chapter 9
Rome burns. Scribonia's wayward daughter. Pleasures of the bath. Nero builds a new palace and garden.

I have named our baby girl Fortunata: Fortunata Annaeus. Fortunata in honour of the goddess that watches over Verriculla and we pray that she smiles on the little one and us all. Our Master has allowed us to bestow his ancestral family name 'Annaeus' upon her. Mistress Paullina, sadly having no surviving children, her only son dying in his youth, is quite joyful with the baby and she points out to her amusement that she played an important role in ensuring the conception. I think I told you about that. Although I think we would have managed, unassisted.

June the 19th will be remembered. A terrifying conflagration has consumed most of Rome. It started in the Circus Maximus, the wooden seating flaring into the night sky. The wind carried flames into the low district, between the Caelian and Palatine hills. Here the tenement buildings are seven stories high and the streets are narrow, just about as wide as your outstretched arms. Only the rats escaped, only the rats were awake at that time of the night. The fire swept around the foot of the Palatine and along the Sacred Way consuming all the fine villas in its path including our former residence.

The awakened populace fled from one district to another, some lifting and carrying the infirm and the aged; mothers dragging their infants behind them, others terrified in the choking smoke trampled down those before them, causing a congestion of the injured in the narrow streets. The fire that followed them would burst out to the side or in front of them due to the intense heat. It is said that some people in their despair surrendered their lives to the flames.

The conflagration defied all efforts to make fire breaks by demolishing buildings. The flames were arrested at the foot of the Esquiline hill six days after it started by the demolition of the whole district; only to start up again in the more open parts of the city, among the temples and pleasure arcades. Great and ancient shrines were burnt and cracked: Servius Tullius' temple to the moon, the great altar and holy place dedicated by Evander to Hercules, the temple vowed by Romulus to Jupiter the Stater, Numa's sacred residence and Vesta's shrine containing Rome's household gods. The spoils of Rome's many victories were lost; great bronze statues by the Greek Masters melted in the heat and marble statues cracked and seared, paintings reduced to ashes. It has been calculated that it is exactly four hundred and eighteen years, four hundred and eighteen months and four hundred and eighteen days since the burning of Rome by the Gauls.[145] Ten of the fourteen districts are now reduced to ashes; they say warm dust is blowing from the city onto the survivors living in the open fields. Nero at Antium, hurried north to Rome as fast as his escort permitted, ordering grain up from the silos of Ostia, food from the surrounding estates, and setting up dole stations to feed the dispossessed.

We have sent food supplies and what we can on the army carts, complete with their escorts to prevent pilfering. Fortune has been good to us again. The master, by abandoning his Roman Villa, has assuredly saved our lives, as our former residence was engulfed in the early

---

[145] 390bc

morning blaze. Our peace here in the country is troubled by thoughts of the fate of our neighbours, the shop keepers and the staff who stayed with the villa.

Nero has done all he can: he has opened up all the public buildings not effected by the fire including the field of Mars and his own gardens where he has constructed emergency shelters for the homeless. He has reduced the price of corn, to a quarter of a sesterce to the pound, to prevent profiteering. The part burnt timber and unusable rubbish is being dumped in the Ostian marshes by the grain barges returning down the Tiber. The new streets are to be broad, set out in blocks, the height of buildings restricted and their fronts set back behind Colonnades. These Nero offered to pay for out of his own purse. Houses are to have a central court yard to facilitate ventilation and prevent the Rome fever. Fronts of buildings should be of Gabii or Alba stone, the partitions should be of brick to minimise the use of timber to prevent the spread of fire. Measures are to be undertaken to improve the public water supply, the old supply had degenerated by the tapping off for private use. All residences are to have readily to hand fire fighting equipment.

The Sibylline books have been consulted and the gods Vulcan, Juno Ceres and Proserpina have been duly propitiated for their fury in allowing Rome to burn.[146] Virtuous matrons were selected for the rites, first at the coast where they collect water to sprinkle the feet of their temple statues on the capital, there they offer up prayers in

---

[146] Sibylline Books: Sybil the prophetess offered nine books to the ancient king Tarquinus of Rome He rejected her offer as too expensive; she burnt three, and then another three, he then agreed the price The books from that time had been consulted by the senate at times of crises Vulcan: ancient god of destructive fire Juno: goddess of marriage and childbirth Ceres: the goddess that sustains man, she provides grain and Proserpina her daughter, who represents rebirth

each temple. Married women with husbands alive joined with them in sacred banquets and vigils. Mistress Paullina not living in Rome was not called upon to join in the religious acts of appeasement; she is accompanying the master on his excursions about southern Italy, where he is writing his 'Letters from a Stoic.' When he has written these he sends them to us for publication. Don't forget your order; I will have special copies prepared in anticipation.

Despite the Emperor's endeavours to placate the populace and the gods by his munificence, ugly rumours have spread amongst the lower orders, that he, Nero, had ordered the city to be burnt. Witnesses claimed that agents of Tiggellinus were seen to be stacking combustible material under the seats of the stadium before the fire started; and it was no coincidence that the fire had rekindled itself on the sixth day, on Tiggellinus' own property. Others said that they had heard that Nero spent all his time performing on his private stage heedless of their incineration, deaf to their cries for help. All utter nonsense, the Emperor was away at Antium, on his return he could not have done more and why would Tiggellinus, devious though he is, burn his own property?

Scribonia's daughter had taken up with a Christian sect and ran away when we moved away from Rome. We assumed to stay with a Christian family; unfortunately they encourage this type of behaviour. As a runaway slave she will have no protection, her mother will now be fraught with worry, the news of the fire will have reached Southern Italy where she is attending her mistress. I have sent agents to look for the girl and provided some notices for them to nail up.

"Runaway slave girl XIIII years old, named Aurelia, property of Annaeus Seneca, usual reward: thought to be with Christians." We have also engaged discreet agents to discover the fate of Paul and his converts. I don't hold out much hope for them.

Our indignant Emperor, out of pique at the populace's ingratitude in not appreciating his efforts to alleviate their hardships, has started work on his new pleasure gardens, stretching down from Augustus's palace complex atop of the Palatine, down to a new artificial lake, then up the Esquiline hill, where he has started the construction of a new palace. These gardens are not to have carefully clipped box hedges laid out in geometrical patterns and lines of pollarded trees, their branches joined to form linear garlands; specimen planting of exotic herbage in regular beds: nature, contorted to man's fancy. Instead, they are to be laid out in a natural imitation of nature.[147] Trees are planted in clusters allowing views to architectural features, and the lake formed naturally in the hollow between the two hills by the damming of a small stream. The lake side is to be planted with water loving plants: irises and lilies, open glades lead down to the lake where small herds of deer, sheep and cattle may be seen ambling down to drink in the twilight of the evening.

A pathway is being constructed through the gardens and around the lake to connect the palace complex on the Palatine, to the new palace on the Esquiline.[148] To facilitate a more pleasing gradient down the Palatine for the imperial litter, a cutting is being made and part of it is to be vaulted to form a tunnel. It emerges at the bottom where our old villa used to be. Statues of gilded bronze are being commissioned to adorn the gardens; their sizes are

---

[147] Capability Brown it seems was not the first to design this form of garden The lake was where the Coliseum now stands

[148] Part of this path down the Palatine is still there The remains of Nero's Esquiline palace also survives, called the Domus Aurea: the golden house

graded and positioned to give the impression of space and distance, as viewed from the imperial path.

The new palace on Esquiline is to have a gigantic gold statue of Nero himself and the palace is to be painted in the new style with pastoral views and gold decoration. That is the reason Nero is bleeding the Empire of both funds and gold. Money sent for the worthy rebuilding of public works, is confiscated to satisfy his grandiose lust for display and luxury. If he was to use the wealth of the Empire to raise armies to subdue the German Tribes across the Rhine, or to force the northern tribes of Britain into subjugation, he would be popular. The contractors here are suffering from severe shortages of labourers, their prices are reaching ridiculous figures; slaves half dead from disease and exhaustion and only fit for death, are coming on to the market, and being sold. Talk is that only a good military campaign with a flood of captives would alleviate these problems, Nero has no interest in the military, other than dressing up in military uniforms.

Artists, artisans and all manner of tradesman have converged on Rome expecting to make a fortune out of the fire. To pay them Nero now strikes forty five denarii to the pound of gold, before it was forty. People complain that they are being cheated by the devaluation; gold statues are an anathema to them, when the currency is debased. Nero, on hearing their complaints, explained to them that gold is the only suitable metal for their Emperor; as like him, it is incorruptible.

The master and mistress are wisely continuing their stay in the South where no mud can stick: no blame accredited to them. Once upon a time, I should have accompanied them, as I once accompanied my master to Rome, but that was years ago. He said,

"Now Cinnamus that you have a family it would be better for you to stay here and look after the villa and our business." The fact is I can now only see to read and write by squinting closely at the scroll. The master is telling me in a kindly way that he prefers a younger man with younger eyes. We could have travelled with them, Verriculla is the neatest scribe in the household, but mistress Paullina forbade it, considering:

"It was too dangerous for the baby."

Our runaway slave, Aurelia, has been returned, not in the condition that she left us. An odious looking person arrived at the villa after dark, he was dressed smartly and had the arthritic look of an old soldier, but smelt of the gutter. He thrust one the notices into the doorman's hand and said,

"Have they recovered the girl?" On hearing that we had not, he continued,

"Will they pay the reward?" The doorman having sent for me,

"They might," I informed him on my arrival and he continued in his disagreeable tone,

"I have found a girl wandering the streets who looks like her, show me the money." I showed him the money, and asked him to,

"Show me the girl."

"All right," he turned and whistled. Along came a female leading another by a rope tied around her neck.

"Hold the light up now, is this the one?"

He took hold of the rope and dragged her head in to the light. She looked gaunt and tired; her hair matted and greasy, it was her though.

"She's cost us a fortune in food and clothes sir; we have come all the way from the city, the reward will hardly cover it, you could perhaps to give us another couple of denarii sir, after all its not your money is it sir?"

"The lying bastard should have a good thrashing if I had my way and the odious female creature too!" The strident voice of Verriculla, in an indignant mood issuing from the shadows behind me, startled them, as it did me. Verriculla continued,

"She's not worth a quarter of what she was"

"Here is half, you get no more, now be off with you." I gave him half the money; the doorkeeper grasped the tether encircling her neck when the villain let go to count the money; and Aurelia was pulled smarty across our threshold back into our ownership, and the door soundly shut. Verriculla organised her immediate ablutions, the burning of her clothes and the feeding of her. She found her quarters with the other women. Later in our room that night I asked my wife what Aurelia had told her?

"All the silly girl will say is that, 'the world shall soon be engulfed in fire when Jesus shall return on clouds of heaven to gather all the faithful to the Lord' the rest of us are to perish in the fire. Jesus only protects the faithful and nothing else matters."

"Sounds like the silly rubbish Paul used to teach. It will never displace the old religion that has made Rome the mistress of the World. She should not have turned from our goddess Fortuna, or kept faith with the Egyptian deities of her mother." Verriculla went over to the cot and smiled down at our baby,

"And in about two weeks she is going to have one of these" She said as she tickled the baby on the cheek. Baby Fortunata responded by throwing her old silver teething ring on to the floor and started to stand up, wobbled and flopped down.

"She loves the walker the carpenter made for her, soon she will be walking on her own." The walker is a little cradle on wheels that baby sits in and then pushes herself along with her feet. Verriculla picked up the baby, held her up to her face and gently brushed their noses together side to side, saying between each action, "we-will-have-to-question-the-silly-girl-in-the- morning, about her condition." For such a charming and pretty act in our own room, I quietly thanked my absent Mistress Paullina for her wisdom in keeping us here together. "What did you say Cinnamus?" I did not tell her the truth. As the baby made baby talking noises, Verriculla smiled and baby Fortunata smiled back.

"I said she has grown, but she is not yet as pretty as her mother, she will have her beautiful blond hair though and her soft white complexion," this, however was the truth.

Late the next morning, it was the day I had designated for the baths to be heated. The master does not take his bath hot, preferring the cold plunge only, but he allows us to used it and heat the water and the hypocaust,[149] as the public baths are too far away. I crept into the bath house; Verriculla was laying face down on the warm slab, her face away from me. The young slave boy attending her had oiled her back, her buttocks and the back of her legs and he was just about to take the strigil to her, when I motioned to him for silence. I stealthily crept over to her and rendered a sharp smack on her smooth oily buttocks, she jerked around, fire in her eyes and venom in her voice, and got out the first syllable of the boy's name, before seeing me.

---

[149] Hypocaust: under floor heating, hot gases from an exterior fire were drawn through cavities under the floor and vented out of the top of the wall cavity

"And, why did you do that, you wicked man."

"Because I like meat tenderised, before I eat it" She rolled back onto her front again and allowed me too bury my face between her cheeks, giving them a not too gentle bite, and then massaged her back, ploughing my writers' thumbs quite hard down each side of her spine and the tips of my fingers running along sides of her ribs gently scratching with my nails and finished off with another slap. Her delicate white skin had turned a lovely shade of pink. The boy helped me strip and we two lovers played our games of amour together in the waters of the bath for an hour or so. With the heat of passion spent, Venus's sweet pervading aura defused, as our lusts were satisfied, her capricious son sought other quarry for his rapturous darts.[150]

Verriculla sent the boy to fetch our baby. We let Fortunata swim between us; she has become surprisingly aquatic and loves the water. The boy dried Verriculla, I dried the baby, then I passed her to Verriculla for feeding and I dried myself. Clean, warm, and well contented, we lounged on the couch Verriculla leaning into my shoulder, nursing baby Fortunata, my arm around her. I asked the boy in pretended seriousness, if he thought the water had made Verriculla as wrinkly as the baby and me. He was delightfully confused to know how to answer and blushed not knowing what to say. My amused wife called him over and gave him a big hug and kiss, and told him not to answer me; and scolded me not to tease the staff. She sent the boy to get some peppermint cordial; it is a refreshing drink after a session in the bath.

---

[150] Amour or Cupid: the son of Venus, goddess of love and equated with causing sexual passion

I took the opportunity to find out what Verriculla had discovered about the returned slave. I don't think it is seemly to discuss the troubles of one slave in front of another. When alone Verriculla told me,

"She blames us for her present misery, says 'We should have left her to die like the others' although she despises us mere hapless tools of her gods, whose judgement will soon condemn us."

"Why us, what have we done." I said this a little too loudly in my indignation.

"I'll tell you her story as far as I can ascertain. But walls have ears, so I'll do it quietly," she said pointedly.

"As you know, she fell out with her mother Scribonia, she had become influenced by a Christian sect and refused to leave Rome telling her mother that she would prefer to be beaten, flayed or even crucified like her saviour, rather than leave her beloved church. The master at the time, you may remember said that, 'Better to let her run away than to feed a malcontent' and If my memory serves me correctly, 'There is little reason to throw good money after bad, she will cost more to recover than she will sell for. She will return when she gets hungry, if she is not too proud'"

"Nothing wrong with your memory," I interjected as she continued.

"And he was right. We get no gratitude for our concern for her safety trying to find her after the fire. She is so stubborn that I doubt if her will could be broken with rods, as it would be in most households. After she ran away she stayed with a woman called the deaconess. She acted as her servant, looking after her family when she was administering church business, or receiving instruction from a certain Bishop Peter, who lived in the same house with his elderly infirm father, called, 'The

Apostle'. He was much venerated for knowing the saviour, but would only say that, 'He is a fisherman' which was thought to prove his holiness. On the morning of the fire, the household awoke to the alarm of the approaching conflagration. The whole household was in a spirit of ecstasy, believing that the promised 'end of time' had come; and their Messiah returned, would gather up the souls of believers and transport them to the gods in heaven. They all fell on their knees imploring the holy flames to consume them. When the crackling fire grew hot about the house the girl took fright, her resolution faltered, and she legged it. The only sensible thing she has ever done in my opinion."

"Saved by fear where common sense had deserted her" I interrupted. Wincing, Verriculla removed the suckling baby from her poor extended nipple, and turned her around to feed on the other side, with mock stern voce, she addressed her little tormentor.

"No chewing with those little sharp teeth or I will chew you!" Verriculla allowed the eager little mouth to suck onto her other nipple. I gently slipped my arm under her arm and supported her tender breast with my cupped hand. With my other I pulled her long hair aside and gently bit the rim of her ear and caressed it with my lips.

"I rather like nibbling you myself" I whispered very quietly into her ear. She turned her head a little and I bent mine just enough to plunge my tongue deep into that pretty orifice.

"There is not one piece of you I don't adore I could nibble you all over"

She wriggled her back into me as she replied soothingly,

"I know, and we both adore you too. You and I were drawn together here from across the world and I have always been lucky since I first left home in faraway Britain. And now I have a beautiful baby and loving husband who gives me all that I desire. Shall I continue, or do you want to continue exploring my ear? Or is that our peppermint cordial coming?"

The boy entered and poured out two beakers. I drank mine with some difficulty. Verriculla was in danger of spilling hers over her naked lap, so I asked the boy to feed her with the drink; he is very good at that sort of thing, not at all clumsy. After he finished Verriculla sent him off to our room for her camomile oil preparation. It is made simply by adding the crushed plants to a small vial of olive oil, leaving for a few months and straining off.

"Let's discusses Aurelia later." I said, "I cannot keep my mind off you at the moment."

The boy returned with the balm.

"Gently, massage around madam's nipple with the balm and use your fingers lightly." I commanded with unnecessary instructions as he was very assiduous about his delicate task. I licked the droplets of the precious milk that had oozed onto my hand and stood up to take the baby. She had abandoned her font of nourishment and was looking a little blue about the mouth with the wind I suspected. I lifted the little body to my shoulder to relieve her of her discomfort; not only wind escaped her, but our little Fortunata expelled a quantity of warm milky vomit down my back; just as well I was unclothed. The boy nipped over with his strigil handy and scraped it off. Verriculla amused at my plight, picked up her breast band to put on.

"One moment madam and I'll be pleased to help you," the boy said hurriedly cleansing my back with oil.

"Quick, the pot. She is about to go!"

A mother's warning; I held her out just in time to avoid another soiling. All finished the boy attended to the baby's dirtied bottom with a linen towel and forgetting about my unfinished back he returned to secure madam's breast band, passing it around her back and tying it snugly under her bosom; leaving me holding the baby.

"Put her on the floor, she won't run away" Verriculla chided my caution with the baby and I pretended vexation at having been only half cleaned.

I duly put the baby on to the warm tessellated floor and as soon as I had straightened my back, she scooted off in the direction of the bath, crawling at first and then she stood up and waddled two strides before plunging into the waters. When the boy fished her out she was most indignant: her little feet and hands pounding the air and her cries echoing around the walls. Her mother now dressed in her tunic, wrapped her in a dry towel, and with the statement,

"You are tired little one," whisked her off to our room.

The boy finished off my back and helped me dress. He had performed his duties well, I gave him a gratuity that reflected the good time we had had, he beamed his gratitude and I went to our room. Verriculla was seated by the cot combing her long golden hair, the baby already asleep. I took the comb from her hand and continued the task, holding the locks as I teased out the tangles. It looks lovely when combed and hangs naturally down to her shoulder-blades, a golden cascading water fall glinting in the morning sun, would not be finer. However, she reserves all this delight for me, keeping it in two tight plaits coiled and pinned under her veil when she is about. She inspected her hair with approval in the polished bronze hand mirror.

"Now we have finished, shall I tell about our ungrateful runaway,"

"Please carry on, come let us lie on the bed," I invited; and we did.

"As you remember, she ran from the consuming flames, the other Christians preferring to remain in expectation of ascending into the realms of the gods in the arms of their returned messiah. She ran from the house, into a maelstrom of people some trying to get a closer look. Others in panic, trying to escape and others still, wailing their lamentations at their losses. Safe beyond these crowds she sat in the road and despaired of her weakness. She sat for a while, and then a woman spoke to her and persuaded her to accompany her to her home. She thought that somehow this common woman was to be an instrument of her God's punishment and his redemption would follow that punishment. She said that the woman was mostly interested in knowing whether she had a man or had been with a man and was pleased when she told her she was a virgin. She called her a poppet and told her how comfortable they would be, living easy in her new home cosy and pleasant. They travelled a long way across Rome, until the girl had no idea where she was when they entered the woman's house: a second floor, one room apartment. They were greeted by an old crone in dirty clothes. She thought she was a fine fish to catch, and a virgin too. 'Daughter, get her something to eat.' Her daughter went off to the baker. 'Now poppet don't be afraid I just want to have a look at you.' The old crone told her lift her clothing and turn around. 'Not a blemish, not a blemish' she muttered, 'now poppet sit back on the table with your feet up, your old mother wants to see if you have any sores'"

Verriculla swung her legs off the bed and sat up and continued,

"The silly girl was hoping to be treated more harshly, in fact she discovered she enjoyed being admired, showing herself off to the friends calling on the two women. Three days later the daughter told her she had found her a new home and she would take her there. The girl hoped for a cruel master who would scourge her. Her hopes rose when she was taken into a crowded tavern. She could hear cries of a young boy, as he was being beaten with rods for not taking his clothes off and crying that he was, 'no slave' and from a good family"

"Poor boy," I interrupted, "stolen from his family and sold illegally to pimps or brothel keepers." Verriculla agreed.

"Yes, it is a shameful business; does it go on in every big city?"

"I am afraid it does. In the city children have to be watched over constantly if they are not to be stolen." Verriculla shuddered, I guess she thought of our little baby Fortunata, I know I did and she continued,

"When her turn came, she too resolved not to remove her clothes and not to co- operate in the expectation of receiving a heaven sent thrashing of contrition. The auctioneer introduced her as 'the best buy of the year: a beautiful young virgin girl." Verriculla considered the term 'beautiful' an example of salesman's hyperbole. I have no opinion on his remarks.

"The buyers parted forming a passage to the centre ring, as it closed behind her she heard their murmurs of expectation, as to her likely value. The auctioneer announced that the exhibit had recently been orphaned by the fire. 'She has white teeth and good breath.' He grabbed her ear and dragged her around the circle; allowing their dirty fingers to pull open her mouth, to examine her teeth and breath. She started to resist, then felt a little piquancy of excitement, all attention was on her and she started submitting willingly to their oral probing and sniffing. When finished, the auctioneer ushered her to the centre of the ring with flicks of his rod and started the bidding. The first bids were rapidly proffered and then they demanded to see 'the goods.'" Verriculla paused and shifted her position on the side of the bed, before continuing with an exasperated voice.

"The girl claimed that a demon had entered her body and was controlling her actions, for she lifted her skirt and removed her tunic against her will. Then she started turning here and there, standing on her toes, lifting her legs, gesticulating lasciviously to each bidder in turn. The bids rose in value, until there were just three bidders left, they ceased bidding; they needed to ascertain the condition of her virginity before pledging their money further. They pushed their way into the inner circle; they laid her on her back, her hips elevated, supported on her elbows and hands, her legs in the air, wide spread for inspection. When I asked her if they saw the demon, she went off into a diatribe on demons and how they are exorcised, and that is the only time you can see them. Christians have no time for humour in their sect, they are far too earnest, it seems. I think the girl just enjoyed the pleasure of exhibiting herself, the demon is the only way she can accept it. She was finally purchased by an old soldier, his face disfigured by scars of combat. He marched her off to the fields of Mars, around her a neck a halter tether.[151]

---

[151] The Fields of Mars: an open space, where, as the name implies, solders were mustered and exercised Nero had allowed temporary accommodation there The Appian Way runs between it and the Tiber

They turned from the Appian Way into a makeshift street lined with old military tents. A large phallus, roughly carved from a tree stump stood at either end of it, with the sign 'Priapus welcomes you'.[152] Prostitutes, young and old, male and female, stood or sat by their respective abodes, enticing the customers with their charms; their owners, with their chastising rods ready to hand, watched, smiled and bantered greedily with the sauntering, apprising clientele. She followed her new owner into a tent with a girl soliciting unsuccessfully outside, supervised by the proprietor's wife, who evidently was in a foul temper. On their approach she cursed the fire for burning her home and the tent for being draughty, she cursed the trade for there was no money about and when she found out how much money he had paid for the girl, she cursed them both.

Aurelia thought that the prospect of receiving her redemption and joining her Christians in the realm of their gods was almost imminently achievable by simple disobedience. Her expectations were again thwarted by her demon. The Proprietor explained to his wife that, when the work men come to rebuild the city under the army's supervision, their pay and contracts will ensure money in abundance, and not many virgins would be on offer. He said,

'Timing is all important my dear. We wait until the fields of Mars are packed with workers and save the picking of our little flower until after the first pay day. Before that we dress her up real pretty and parade about the town to whet their appetites. Meantime, we can still do

---

[152] Priapus: A god of sex and lust His sacrificial animal was appropriately a donkey or ass

business using Proseda,[153] and the new girl can learn the tricks by watching from behind the curtain.'

Aurelia and her demon were duly ensconced behind the curtain that divided the front from the back of the tent, enjoyed the varied, fascinating, and often funny spectacle displayed before her. She noted that some customers enjoyed beating Proseda with a rope end as part of their pleasure. The proprietor would step in at her cries and complain at the bruises ruining his business, not allowing them to continue until after a satisfactory recompense. She thought her Gods would expel her demon this way. She also noted that she was given a good share of Proseda's food.

The wife gave her every consideration: she washed and scented her body and applied a little make-up, she styled her dark hair around flowers of silver; she clothed her in a tunic so fine that her young body beneath was more alluring than if she were naked. Thus attired and clutching her twigs of Laurel, she was paraded wherever men gathered;[154] and her demon aroused delight within her. Twenty days before the day of her defloration, a board was set up before the tent. On it were written the names of the clientele who wished to be the first. They paid a fee to have their name and their bid added to the list, the magnitude of the bid represented the order of precedence to the virgin.

Clients on placing or replacing bids would be allowed an inspection to confirm the condition of virginity, for consideration of money, although they were never allowed to touch. 'The demon' had made Aurelia

---

[153] Proseda: a name given to girls who stand before their abode, soliciting
[154] The Laurel, to show she was a virgin

forget her punishment and her gods and made her love flattery attention and excitement."

The story being longer than I expected, I interrupted Verriculla, to ask her to make shorthand notes for me to write up later. She took the opportunity to walk over to baby, making sure she was safely tucked up, she cooed down at it, touching its little British nose.

"Sleeping soundly my little one, you've had a busy day haven't you," She came over to the bed and pulled me off it and we re-seated ourselves in the usual chair, Verriculla in her favourite position on my lap, her arm around my neck, my arm across her lap clasping her thigh. Thus seated, she continued her story of Aurelia, and her doubtful demon.

"Two nights before the lamp[155] was to be extinguished the proprietor killed his Proseda, she had been unable to work despite repeated lashings, she lay on the ground writhing in agony, crying and holding her womb, swollen with child. The wife told the husband to put her away quickly. The girl pretended to be asleep, she saw the husband pin the proseda to the ground with his knee and constrict her neck with both hands. He took the cadaver and threw it on the rubbish heap to be collected in the morning.[156]

That night the girl thought of her own demise and was hopeful that her subsequent salvation through her god was close and she would eventually suffer the same treatment as the last proseda. A message from her god whispered by an angel, told her he had not forsaken her.[157] That morning Aurelia was given special attention, they called her their lovely new Proseda. They were pleased

---

[155] Lamps outside bordellos, denoted a virgin had been acquired
[156] It is quite in order to kill ones slaves under Roman law
[157] Angel: messenger from the Gods

with the money their new Proseda was generating; the list had grown to over thirty clients bidding to ascend the list. The next day they were to gather in their spoils. When the time came for the defloration, the clients gathered out side the tent. Some of them hadn't turned up, but it was still a good turn out. A rather corpulent and elderly butcher was at the head of the list, and proudly stepped forward when he was announced 'the highest bidder' he was pleased, as he was also demonstrating his wealth. Then a late comer stood before him and raised his bid. He objected. The newcomer's offer was not exceeded; he paid his money over and the aggrieved butcher waited his turn, second in the queue. As they entered the tent, Aurelia felt his small ringed fingers press through the fine fabric dress and slide over her buttocks, pulling the thin fabric tight against her so all could see. Then turning and calling back to the envious faces.

'This little pearl is mine, do come in and watch if you like.'

The demon that thrilled her out side went into ecstasy, when the man very slowly lifted her tunic above her head, under the hushed lascivious gaze of the onlooker's eyes, in the crammed tent. When in turn Aurelia stripped him the surprise that he intended was that he was a she. Aurelia performed magnificently to the joy of all present. The lamp was not extinguished, but the lady was satisfied, and the butcher, demoted to second place, still had the virgin he hoped for. Well, he should have done, but unfortunately he had overexcited himself at the previous display and was unable to recover sufficiently before the water had emptied."[158]

---

[158] A reference to a water-clock: a vessel with a small hole at the bottom allowing water to empty; thus gauging time

Verriculla, did relate to me further details of the proceedings that day, However, I shall not bore you with the tedium of them, but she did tell me that,

"After a time the girl's demon became less potent and she was able to set her mind again on thoughts of her religion. As time passed, her owners treated their diminishing asset with less care and more cruelty and soon started expelling the demon with beatings. She considered that at last, her prayers were about to be fulfilled when her master came back with a new girl: a new proseda, she expected to shortly to ascend to her gods in the manner of her predecessor, her confinement becoming due." Unfortunately for her, her master had noted her perverse religious mutterings and guessed she was the runaway slave of our advert and stayed his hand in the hope of extracting the last bit of profit from her, the reward."

Chapter 10
A revolt of gladiators. Naval catastrophe. Death in the house of Seneca. Verriculla assumes authorship.

It was a mistake to pay the reward. Aurelia was sullen and refused to do the simplest task, disdaining work in a pagan household, but she ate our food. Irritated by her ungrateful attitude, I told her to run away back to her Christian friends to have her baby, which she did entirely without hindrance from us. Before she went she desecrated the larium, she threw out the votive icons of the personal gods of our household including our goddess Fortuna, and chalked a chi-rho all over it.[159]

It is understandable why these sects are not liked, and that girl and her baby have probably gone to their doom. After she left, I heard that riots had erupted in Rome and many of these initiates received the death they craved for and predicted: they were burnt as human torches. Although we are looking forward to the expected arrival of our master and mistress, it is not going to be easy to explain matters to Scribonia, Aurelia's mother and the mistress's maid. I know the master will not begrudge the money spent on her; he will say, "It was well meant."

The old town of Praeneste, about twelve miles south west of Rome, where the great temple of Fortuna Primgenia occupies the whole of one side of the hill, has experienced a break out of gladiators.[160] The air there is

---

[159] A monogram of the Greek letters chi and rho, the first two letters in Christ's name

[160] Fortuna Primgenia: a case of two deities of similar nature, melding together in one shrine Fortuna is particularly worshiped by Cinnamus and Verriculla The town is now called Palestrina Remains of the temple were discovered after 2nd world war bombing The whole complex occupies terraces to the top of the hill

known for its coolness in summer. Consequently the surrounding area is studded with villas of the rich wishing to escape the stifling summer heat of Rome. Fortunately, it being late in the year, they had returned to Rome. The gladiators failed to apprehend any worthwhile hostages; they were soon rounded up and re-incarcerated by the army without harm to the temple, the priests or the devotees. When our master returns I will request permission to travel there to consult the oracle on our baby's future. The people of Rome took fright as they always do, fearing the worst and expecting another Spartacus, but it was all a storm in a wine cup. Much more serious was the storm out at sea. The Navy had orders to winter at Misenum; they had been stranded at Formiae by the heavy seas. Nero insisted that his orders be carried out and the fleet return to Misenum, despite the weather the fleet set out in the face of the heavy on-shore winds. Trying to round Cape Misenum they were driven aground near Cumae.[161] Nero lost many ships and lives to Neptune through his intransigence. The navy however, has lost none to Mars, as peace continues across the seas.

The shock of the death of our former Master Seneca has devastated my husband, he feels unable to inform you himself of the plot and its consequences. He has requested that I, Verriculla, should do so. Cinnamus has always maintained that men of renown and talent that inhabit imperial circles, will inevitably die at the behest of the Emperor, and that few Emperors die in peace. Few men have survived the machinations and foibles that surround Emperors for as long as our Master Seneca did. However, Cinnamus had expected the fatal command and he

---

[161] Misenum: the home port of the fleet, it is where Pliny the Elder set out to rescue victims of the erupting Vesuvius that engulfed Pompeii and Herculaneum

thought he was prepared for it, but alas, as he says after forty years....

It happened two days after the master and mistress returned from the south. Seneca looked frail and tired; illness had caused him to return. He was at dinner with his Doctor and Cinnamus when Gavius Silvanus an officer of the Guard and the Emperors' messenger, but not an angel, was announced.[162] He read out the Imperial statement.

"Antonius Natalis has confessed to conveying a request from the self-confessed traitor Piso, that he, Piso, should visit you. The reason for this request was to discuss his plot to kill the Emperor."

Our master Seneca spoke in a kindly voice to put the troubled herald at his ease,

"Please tell our good friend and noble poet the Emperor Nero that I did receive a request from Piso to visit me; it was refused, owing to the declining condition of my health. Piso made no further request; I naturally assumed he was sniffing around hoping to get a mention in my will, forgetting that I have already given most of it to my former pupil and Emperor. He is an example of the problems that beset us men of wealth, or past wealth, when approaching the Styx.[163] Now you must take refreshment dear Silvanus, and tell all the information you can."

"Sir, two weeks ago a naval officer from Misenum: Volusius Proculus reported to Tiggellinus and Nero, that a woman had solicited him in an attempt to persuade him to

---

[162] Nero, considered himself a god, as did many of his subjects also, Angels are messengers from the gods Verriculla may be having a dig at the Christians as well

[163] Styx: The mythical river that is necessary to cross at death to enter the underworld Seneca is trying to avoid an unnatural death by claiming he is about to expire naturally; a ploy he has used before

recruit his fellow officers into a plot to assassinate the Emperor at sea. Volusius Proculus reflected on the debacle when Nero tried to murder Agrippina at sea; he had been a part of it; he had the woman arrested and delivered to Tiggellinus. The woman had heard Proculus complaining that he had not received a reward for his part in the Agrippina debacle, subsequently she suspected his loyalty. Tiggellinus kept this woman, Epicharis, in detention. On questioning her, she denied all. She was of low birth, an ex-slave and not rich, he probably mistakenly considered her an imbecile."

Seneca smiled.

"A clever woman," he muttered, "then if she stayed mum, who accuses me?" Seneca indicated to the waiting servant to refill Officer Silvanus' cup.

Paullina and I had been eating together in the adjacent room, on the arrival of the Imperial messenger we entered the room through the connecting doorway and stood behind Seneca's couch, so as to observe all. Refreshed, and with the strong wine loosening his tongue, Silvanus continued.

"Flavious Scaevinus gave the game away, or his head freedman Milichus did so, doubting his master's competence to perform a decisive act of regicide; wine over the years having dulled his master's limited abilities. He gauged his best advantage lie in spilling the beans and claiming a reward. Scaevinus had taken the old sacrificial dagger from the Temple of Fortune and instructed Milichus to sharpen it. He made no attempt to conceal his intentions: he made out his will, he boasted of his intended action to his household, and as usual, he was drunk. This freedman of Scaevinus, after the subsequent arrests, tried to assuage his duplicity by blaming his conduct on his over ambitious nagging wife. They also arrested Antonius

Natalis, a crony of Silvanus; Tiggellinus' interrogated them separately. For an easy death the whole plot was soon revealed. Gaius Calpurnius Piso was named as the leader, and to be the future Emperor. You were suspected Seneca, owing to the previous rumour of a plot with Piso."

"No doubt my good friend," Seneca interrupted, "and they will have arrested Antonius Natalis, he and Piso spilled much wine together and had no secrets from each other, nor any from Nero either now. Tiggellinus will take advantage of the plot to rid himself of all the men who may in the future supplant him, when he too, vies to become Emperor. My nephew Lucan too will be implicated as Nero is jealous of the warm praise he is receiving from the public for his latest epic; the public have also misconstrued certain lines in praise of Nero as a satire on him.[164] That boy never could endure pain; he will incriminate his own mother at the sight of the torturer's implements."

"I am afraid you are right Seneca, he did just that, he did offer to implicate his mother before Nero." For the first time I noticed Seneca bow his head in dejection as Silvanus spoke; Paullina gripped his shoulder and he immediately regained his affable persona beneath his intense concentration. With a sharp almost imperceptible glance he had Silvanus' cup refilled.

"He was not the only one, they all confessed and incriminated whoever Tiggellinus wanted them to: senators, knights, army commanders Tiggellinus has used the occasion to rid himself of Faenius Rufus so as to gain complete control of the guard,[165] only those currently in his or Nero's favour can sleep easy. There has been,

---

[164] Lucan's Pharsalia, book one 70-129
[165] Rufus, you may remember, is joint commander of the Praetorian Guard with Tiggellinus

however, one person whose behaviour has been exemplary and she is the freed-woman Epicharis. Tiggellinus renewed his interest in her when the plot was exposed. Despite being whipped, burned with hot irons and having her limbs racked, she defied and scorned her torturers. The next day, when she was being taken on a cart for further examination, her legs unable to support her after her racking, she untied her breast-band and secured it around her neck and also to a ring on the cart that prisoners are normally shackled to. Her oppressors to their chagrin were thwarted, when she threw herself off the cart and crossed the Styx. How different her noble and glorious death to that of Faenius Rufus, he tried to maintain his position, although a member of the plot, by rounding up and prosecuting his fellow conspirators. When Subrius Flavious tried to assassinate Nero at Rufus' agreed signal, during the trial of Julius Augurinus at which Rufus was prosecuting; Rufus prevented him! A wicked act that failed to save him, Tiggellinus had him already marked for elimination."

Silvanus knew no more, he could tell no more, he offered commiserations to Seneca and departed a little unsteadily.

We all looked to Seneca and he voiced what we all thought, he said,

"When I was a young man I was afflicted severely by onslaughts of the disease that constricts the breathing. These bouts lasted for about an hour and each painful effort to suck in air, I thought was my last. That is why our good friend the doctor here, calls it 'rehearsing death' since, sooner or later a painful breath will be just that. Death has had many tries at throwing me out of this world ever since, and yet death is only a return to the same condition I was in before I was born, just as a lamp is as dark before it is lit, as it is when it is put out. What does it matter then when you are born or when you die. The man to admire and imitate, is he who finds joy in each day and in spite of that is not reluctant to die. Nero will not allow death to throw me out like a reluctant guest, but allow me a dignified and willing departure from life. I urge my friends and my ever faithful wife Paullina, therefore, not to waste their precious days on grieving after my death; it will benefit me not. All I ask is a small pyre to burn this frail old carcass. Look at it, it is already devoid of flesh, just saggy skin and bone, it's not worth a good blaze."

We smiled through our tears.

"Now I must ask Verriculla if she would be so kind as to fetch my will"

I left to fetch it. When I returned Paullina was on her knees hugging her husband's legs declaring her determination to share his funeral pyre, Cinnamus, equally disconsolate was on his knees hugging Paullina saying that,

"He could not bear to lose her too."

Seneca calmed them down and dictated to me the adjustments to his will. As his nephew and brother had, or were expected to suffer the same fate, there was no reason to include them. He asked me to record the proceedings of that day in my best shorthand, so as to ensure he conducts himself in accordance with his philosophical studies.[166] Seneca instructed that water should be heated for the bath and asked his good friend and doctor, Annaeus, to take charge of the poison he kept for such an occasion and continued to speak in a relaxed mood to calm our fears.

---

[166] Seneca, it appears is sensitive to the charge of hypocrisy A charge levelled at him during his life and ever since, owing to the high position he achieved and his great wealth, a formidable part of which was gained by usury

"Attalus used to say when I was a youth,[167] 'Man should strive to become king of himself, achievable by poverty showing us that everything we had that was beyond the needs of life, was an unnecessary burden encumbering us.' When he exposed our pleasures, not only the illicit, but the unnecessary ones as well, I was tempted on walking out to give up my wealth for a happier life. This is the reason that I refrain from wine. When we see the madness and misery it induces in others, we know Attalus is right. And also the glutton that spews up one helping, to gorge another into his distended stomach, is a fool to his craving and his health. Likewise I gave up the use of scent, as a clean body has no smell. Hot baths, I believe, are conducive to effeminacy, exercise is a far healthier method of generating a sweat, rather than stewing in hot water and steam. Although later tonight I may well break the habits of a lifetime and indulge in a hot tub, with the blessing of our Emperor." Spoken with a wry smile,[168] "Sotion used to tell us that Sextius refused to eat meat on the grounds that man had food enough to sustain him, without shedding blood.[169] When men took to the tearing flesh, it became a pleasure to him; so the habit of cruelty was formed. He also argued that increasing the range of diet encouraged gluttony and was alien to our being and health. When I was Nero's tutor I tried to instil all these virtues into him for his own benefit and that of the Empire. My success, alas, proved limited."

The last syllable of his joke he made with a very wry smile and a resigned theatrical gesture of the trained orator. "Gavius Silvanus will return presently with either

---

[167] Attalus: otherwise unknown, presumably a stoic teacher practicing in Spain
[168] A hot bath to increase blood pressure, to aid the expected suicide
[169] Sextius Quintus: a late first century b.c Roman eclectic philosopher, influenced by Stoic and Pythagorean ideas

a reprieve or not. If I am to die in my own time, in my own way, in my own house and in the company of friends and well-wishers; how could fortune treat me better? To be free of this old illness racked body, is to return to the state I was in before I was born, whether that was conscious or not it will be a blessing. If fortune decrees that I should live on to see the sun's light and feel his heat once more, that too would be fortune's blessing, as I should continue to enjoy the simple pleasures, the conversation of my friends and the love of my good wife, Paullina. Therefore, dread not the arrival of our messenger Gavius Silvanus; for he must bring us good news." Thus the short hours passed; we had the couches moved closer together than usual when the food table was removed, Paullina reclined close to her husband holding his hand, his frail body propped with bolsters, Annaeus Status held the other hand, or I think more correctly his wrist, as he monitored his pulse. I was propped on the couch opposite taking notes, Cinnamus next to me one hand gripping my leg the other stroking Paullina's knee; the staff eagerly attentive.

When Gavius Silvanus returned, Seneca greeted him in the manner of a bearer of good tidings. Enquiring after the health of the Emperor, Silvanus cautiously replied that,

"The Emperor is in his usual condition.[170] Poppaea and Tiggellinus were anxious to learn of your reaction to the news. They were taken aback when I told them of your calm reaction and confident speech. Only Nero smiled sadly, I repeat his words,

'Tell the dear old thing that I shall miss him, neither of us wanted to be Emperor; would that my Mother had been I.'"

---

[170] Inebriated probably

He held his hand to his forehead as he almost whispered this. There was a long pause and he continued in a stronger voice,

"Paullina needn't die; take Acte with you to comfort her."

"That is the reason for my delay, my escort and I waited for her. I am instructed to stay here so that I may report your death."

Acte entered the room on the conclusion of Silvanus' speech. She seemed to complete the scene for the coming drama.

Seneca lent forward as if to gather up strength, he quietly pleaded that,

"Tears of grief should be quickly abated and the clothes of mourning soon replaced. Fortune will love you more for doing so, and it won't affect me a jot. A simple stoic's funeral is all I ask."

Paullina refuted him saying,

"With our only son dead as he gained the threshold of manhood, dying in the arms of your mother Helvia;[171] I shall be left without a reason to live. Therefore the best and proper action to avoid grief is for me to die with you."

Seneca rose with the aid of a servant.

"My dear if that is what you wish, I shall not argue. Come friends my good doctor has tasks to perform."

Arm in arm with Paullina, a servant supporting the other elbow, their heads held high, they made their slow and inexorable exit into the bedroom. Surrounded by friends and devoted staff, the elderly couple lay side by side on their bed, their legs raised on a bolster, each with an arm hanging down the side of the bed ready to receive the scalpel. Beneath, ready on the floor to receive the

---

[171] Seneca's only child died at the age of 14

drippings of their warm blood, silver bowls were placed. Annaeus Statius with his back to the bed, so as not to reveal his steel scalpel to the victims, stropped it sharp. With it he knelt at the side of Seneca. His assistant, a slave who always attended him, twisted a cord around Seneca's upper arm. The doctor bent the wrist back and made the incision. Seneca's body went rigid with pain and Paullina lent over and wiped the sweat from his brow, as the blood dripped. I think it was worse for Paullina, she had just witnessed the pain of Seneca lying so close, and anticipation heightens fear. Bravely she encouraged the doctor to proceed with the incision of death.

Scribonia bathed their faces with cool lavender water to sooth them and dispel the odour of fear, sweat, and of sweet blood. The thin body of Seneca refused to relinquish the fluid of life, despite the doctor's efforts to enlarge the wound. The doctor stood him up and walked him about. He tried cutting arteries in the other wrist and on the ankles too. All this caused Seneca to voice his distress and pain, and not wishing to add his own trauma to that of his wife, he pleaded that she should be taken into an adjoining room. Scribonia immediately seized the opportunity to bandage her mistresses' wound on the pretext that her mistress, would not like to cause a mess on the floor, we can take it off when we get there. We all knew she would not; not at least until her mistress had recovered. We were all approving and grateful for her loyal disobedience. When Paullina had left, Seneca asked for a drink and proposed the time had come to find out if the taste of hemlock is to his liking.[172] The doctor dripped the extract into a cup of the pure spring water that Seneca

---

[172] Hemlock: a poisonous herb of the umbelliferae family It has a sedative action closing down the nervous system

habitually drank. He used to joke that he only drank pure water, so that he would taste it if his enemies tried to poison him. He drank it down as bravely as Socrates.[173] As the drug reduced the pain of his injuries he became more lucid, when asked what hemlock tasted like he replied.

"It is bitter and tastes rather like mice, or more like the way a mouse nest smells, if you are offered a drink of mouse-nest soup I recommend you refuse it. Mice on the other hand are quite tasty. I feel much better for that drink."

The Doctor told him,

"Like Socrates, you will lose the feeling in your feet and hands and when the drug reaches the heart; the end."

Although his voice and limbs were weak from loss of blood, his mind never failed as he engaged us in conversation. Until he suddenly remembered his bath,

"My bath, my bath, I have forgotten."

I think if he could, he would have raised a hand in an oratorical gesture but his hand was as weak as his voice.

"I have not had a hot one for 40 years, now dear slaves, now is the time; but how is my poor wife?"

Doctor Statius assured him that although Paullina had lost plenty of blood she would recover and was now sleeping soundly.

"Then if you will, dear slaves, place me beside her for a short wile, so as I may touch her with my face, for it is the only part of me that still has feeling."

---

[173] Socrates: Athenian philosopher, he was condemned to death for not recognising the Athenian gods Some scholars argue he was given the opportunity to escape, but he carried out the sentence administering hemlock to himself According to his student Plato he admonished his friends for weeping, although they said that "they were weeping for themselves suffering his loss," Socrates replied that, "he had sent the women away to avoid such a scene" Socrates died in 399bc at the age of 70

Two slaves carried him gently to the sleeping body of Paullina, they placed him next to her, face to face, and draped his blood caked hand over her shoulder.

Cinnamus and I stood close together, silent, our arms entwining, tears once more washing our cheeks, not because of the ensuing tragedy but because they were beautiful, serene: the Master heading towards death; the Mistress towards life. I thought back to the time when my father and I parted and of his fate among my dreadful relations. Acte came up and stood close behind us, her comforting soft warm bosom pressing onto my back, her warm tears wetting my shoulder as she gently caressed the back of Cinnamus' neck. Seneca lay there for a while, looking into his wife's face and then reached forward and touched his lips to her lips. His validation to his sleeping wife now over, he called to be taken to the bath. There he fell silent, to speak no more. When the doctor was satisfied that the pulse had stopped, Cinnamus said,

"The world will know him by his writings; but we have lost a friend."

The funeral was very quiet. There were no professional mourners tearing their clothes, covering themselves with ashes and wailing lamentations, the ancestral masks were not paraded; there were no games or entertainment.[174] He was the last of his family, as there is no hope for his brothers and nephew; he, who had brought Rome for a few short years under Nero, to a peak of wealth and peace; had few who dared to mourn him.

---

[174] Masks were made of the deceased and kept in a special room, at funerals they were taken out and worn by people to represent the ancestors of the newly deceased Games had been inaugurated in the past as part of the funeral In very ancient times a slave was sacrificed, later two slaves were pitted against each other to determine the sacrifice These bouts became ever more elaborate, spectacular and politically important, evolving into the huge gladiatorial games

Nero's reputation could only decline without Seneca's moral guidance; Nero's tragedy assured.

Chapter 11
Acte and Julius move in. Dido's gold, a tail of credulity. Nero performs. The death of Poppaea. Cinnamus goes to Liguria. Various demises. Paullina's revelations.

Acte now stays with us whenever Nero is absent from Rome; for she now tends him more in the role of a nurse, or even as a surrogate mother, than that of a concubine, and sooths his troubles in his darkest hours after the courtly sycophants, mistresses and even the empress Poppaea have subverted his mind, preying on his fears and weaknesses. Nero has asked for his only son, Acte's son, to be hidden secretly away from the court and those who would make him Emperor; Nero believes that all other men are happier than emperors, and safer than emperors. When Acte told him that he was staying in old Seneca's villa, with Paullina, Cinnamus and me, Nero's frenzied mind gained some relief. He still remembered me as the little blond girl from Britain, who was lucky and predicted her tribe's loyalty. It is strange the things that emperors remember when so many troubles apparently assail them. Thus, in a way, Fortunata has acquired an older brother and a lovely aunt. Acte calls him Julius after Nero's family name, there are plenty of people who have taken their name from the house of Julian over the years so it will not arouse comment from the curious. The addition of Julius to our house has certainly revived Cinnamus. The loss of our master seemed to draw all the life out of him. He took longer to recover than Paullina. She has her scars, but conducts herself with dignity and now has a smile for even the most menial slave. Cinnamus talks to the children in Greek, telling them the old stories he learnt as a child, although they are too young to understand, he believes that it is important for them to grow up understanding the languages of the empire. He even encourages me to speak British to them; not a thing I do in company, you understand.

There has been a lunatic Carthaginian named Caesellius Bassus staying in Rome. He has been enjoying the food at rich men's tables on the account of a dream he had. On his estate there is a very deep cave, the entrance being covered over by earth being piled on top of it. At the bottom of the cave, lie piles of ancient gold bullion, stacked high like columns. The dream also revealed that the Phoenician Queen Dido had hidden the gold in fear that it would corrupt her young men. Now the sons of Aeneas, the rich and greedy of Rome, listened fearing they may miss an opportunity of gaining greater wealth, and worse, their friends might pre-empt them; whereas Aeneas was content with gathering the lovely Dido into his arms.[175] Nero got to hear of Bassus' dream and like the rest of Rome caring nought for the risk of corruption, sent a naval detachment to Carthage with Bassus, in high expectation of recovering a fortune. When the time of the second Neronian Games arrived, the talk was of the expected arrival of Dido's gold.[176] Nero had no problem borrowing money from the credulous and greedy to fund his Games, against the expected arrival of Dido's hoard, offering them high rates of interest.

---

[175] Virgil in his poem "The Aeneid" tells us that, after the sack of Troy, Aeneas led the dispossessed Trojans to Carthage There Queen Dido befriends the Trojans and falls in love with Aeneas, who deserts her and sails off to establish a new kingdom in Italy: Rome Romans, therefore considered themselves of Greek origin

[176] Games not only included sports as we think of them but also competitions in poetry, music and reciting the performers own works Nero, we suspect, preferred the latter categories

Performers at the competition directed their panegyrics to Nero, along the lines that 'Nero's reign is truly golden; the earth now brings forth not only crops of golden wheat, but gold itself.' On the pretext of averting the degrading spectacle of Imperial feet treading the boards of the common stage, shamelessly bringing the whole Empire into contempt, the senate offered Nero in advance the prize for song and to confer upon him the crown for eloquence. It was of no avail. The emperor was insistent, castigating them for favouritism. Acte thought the whole thing very funny when she told us all this. Nero considers his musical accomplishments as near divine as himself, so that to deprive the people of his performance, he considers an act of sacrilege.

The weary senators were forced day and night to watch and listen to all the performances. When Nero performed, spies watched the faces in the audience for those that showed a lack of rapture. Vespasian actually fell asleep, he found conquering Britain apparently less exhausting, but fate was kind to him, he got away with it saying, 'I am only a bumpkin horse trader, overpowered by the closeness of divinity.' All the soldiers love the old veteran campaigner and enjoyed his irony. To his good fortune it was lost on Tiggellinus.[177]

The people from the old conservative country towns, unfamiliar with the need to harmonise their clapping with the more expert and urbane applauders, caused disharmony. The guardsman positioned in the aisles used their rods to engender rhythmic clapping in the less skilful, until harmonious synchronisation was achieved. When Nero had finished reciting his poetry, certain

---

[177] Just as they were to make him Emperor, in 69ad when he was campaigning in the Jewish War Now he was earning a living as a horse trader

members of the audience called upon him to show them all his accomplishments. He returned later with his cithara.[178] It is not that he is a bad performer, as you know I have heard him myself, he once gave me a private performance, although, I will confess I am no judge. He observes the performer's etiquette scrupulously I am told; he never sits while performing; nor does he blow his nose or spit on the stage and to wipe away his perspiration he uses nothing but his own clothes and he does it all himself. At the conclusion of the contest, he lines up with the other competitors on bended knee offering both gestures of deference to the public and in humble trepidation to the judges. Nero, as you have guessed, won all the prizes and the speculators lost their money: Dido's gold was just a dream.

This has been a sad year for deaths. Tiggellinus' purges have ravaged the noble families of their best men and where he has failed, plague has done its best and as usual not being particular as to the rank of its victims. Fortunately, Acte is in Campania still consoling Nero after the death of the Empress Poppaea. Campania is free of plague, but has been subjected to severe storm damage, less dangerous than the plague, I think you will agree. There have been all the usual rumours going around about Poppaea's death: that she was poisoned; that Nero kicked her in a drunken tantrum causing her to abort her baby and she died as a result. Acte has now told me that while Poppaea was performing as a priestess of Isis, carrying the sacred Nile Water of life, she collapsed in pain onto the floor. Desperately she tried not to spill the water, but the sacred vessel smashed on to the marble floor and as a

---

[178] Cithara: a seven stringed instrument with a larger sound box than a lyre, used for professional performances

result of losing the fertile water, in great pain she miscarried and died. She was a woman of cruelty and vindictiveness. Many an orphan or widow will secretly smile at her demise, and sneer at Nero's funeral oration praising her virtues and beauty. Her body was embalmed in the Egyptian fashion and entombed in the Mausoleum of Augustus.

Cinnamus is travelling north to Liguria to buy some property. He is very secretive about it, he won't tell me where it is, or who is selling it.

Your master is very wise retiring to Butrint; keeping away from Rome may have its cultural drawbacks, but in the present climate it is far healthier than Rome.[179] Cinnamus considers that it must be a very fine city, as it is of Greek origin, and has a very fine Greek Theatre set on top of a round hill. They might put on performances of our late master's plays. The city on the lower slopes is nearly surrounded by water, as a sea-way flows into a large blue lake beyond, offering a safe harbour and ensuring a pleasant coolness even on the hottest days, so it is healthier there in every way. When you are tired of Butrint you can take a ship and sail the ten miles west to visit the great library at Apollonia. Another fine example of Corinthian architecture; or if we have furnished you with all your literary needs, sail across the straits to Corcyra.[180] The most important deity in Butrint is Asclepius; your continuing good health is therefore assured.[181] How Cinnamus knows all this is a mystery, for he claims he has never been there, but he speaks with conviction.

---

[179] Buthrotum: Butrint on the Albania Coast adjacent to Corfu

[180] Corcyra: now better known by its Venetian name, Corfu Butrint and Apollonia are in modern Albania

[181] Asclepius: the Greek god of healing His principle cult centre was at Epidaurus in the Peloponnese He is depicted in art carrying a staff with a snake coiled around it His constellation is Ophiuchus, the serpent holder

Servius Orfitus has proposed to the senate that three months of the year are to have new names: April is to be called Neroneus, May- Claudius and June- Germanicus. Therefore, when you write to tell us of your pending arrival at your new home, be sure not to confuse the month: June is now considered unlucky as two senators of the Junii family have been executed. Therefore, better to arrive in Germanicus, although June is Germanicus under a different name, and Germanicus was of the house of Junii. Time will tell if these proposals are accepted, but it seems unlikely.[182]

It is hard to give you good news, the talk in Rome and all Italy is of the casualties of the latest purge. Can you bear one more dolorous report on the latest victim? He is Nero's authority on matters of good taste in all things: Publius Petronius Niger.[183] He was close to Nero, witty, popular, a good business man and an honest governor of Bithynia; hedonism being his main vice. As to questions of taste, whether it be on art, architecture, gastronomy, wine or manners, all were arbitrated by Petronius Niger, who preferred the exquisite to the trivial and the elegant to the mundane. He championed the new style of house decoration; walls were to be painted with natural country views of the owner's villas and farms. An urbane Senator, he enjoyed regular literary and philosophical discussions in the company of Nero, and my Master Seneca, his brother and nephew Lucan and the most gifted writers of our age. All now crushed by the power of Tiggellinus and his faction. The Emperor was still in Campania and

---

[182] We know they did not Nor did the next dynastic house introduce their own names, otherwise our months would be called, Vespasian, Titus, Domitian and Flavius The Roman calendar did not have weeks

[183] This is the same Petronius spoken of in the earlier letter concerning 'the barking dog mosaic' in his comic story of misadventure 'The Satyricon'

Petronius was on his way to join him there. When he had reached Cumae, where he owned a villa, he received the order to arrange his own death. He had a nocturnal habit of sleeping through the day and being active at night. That evening he gathered his friends about him, severed his own veins and started a light discourse with his friends and listened to their reciting of comedies and other amusements. From time to time he bound up his wounds, reopening them later as fancy took him. He made out his will, giving gifts and punishments to his slaves as he thought fit. To Nero and Tiggellinus he dared to give nothing, shunning the usual flatteries.[184] Although, to the Emperor he sent under seal a detailed list of Nero's sexual improprieties. Nero agitated and disappointed, he was expecting a legacy, blamed Silia, the wife of a senator, a friend of Petronius and a confidant of the Imperial bed chamber for telling the lubricious details. Petronius then had his signet-ring broken to prevent it sealing the death of his friends in the hands of forgers. He allowed himself to become sufficiently weak that during the dinner he started to doze and then died. Giving the appearance of a natural death; Petronius did every thing with style.

Paullina has now completely recovered from her ordeals, and is playing the role of grandmother to Julius and Fortunata. With Cinnamus doting on them and Acte as well when she can get away from court, I feel they are in danger of receiving far too much attention. I do know how lucky they are to have Paullina as a grandmother, rather than my own back in barbarous Britain. Paullina now takes a little wine with us in the evening, and I have

---

[184] Flatteries and bequests were made to the Emperor and persecutor for allowing them to commit suicide, thus keeping their will legal and their families safe If executed the Emperor took all, leaving the family destitute Petronius has defied and spurned the system

also enticed her into the pleasures of the hot baths and our ever diligent attendant. She felt guilty at first, but the feeling of a little naughtiness heightens her pleasure, when succumbing to the attentions of the masseur.

Today is a special anniversary for us, Cinnamus has decreed it so. It is the anniversary of my purchase. We have had a little party with our friends and how nice, Acte was able to come too. At dinner between the courses we had acrobats, musicians, singers and comedians whose buffoonery gave us all a good laugh, aided I must say by more than a little wine and our cook makes wonderful ice cream and fruit jelly.

Dear old Cinnamus made a little speech,

"Other people have birthdays" he said, "but as for our dear Verriculla her birthday is unknown and in a way when she came into the house of Seneca, she was re-born into a new world, so let that day be her birthday."

It is too embarrassing to relate all the sweet and charming things he and the others said about me.

It is late now and I am the last one awake, the others have all fallen asleep on the couches, the servants have covered them over where they lay. All is still; I write with the light of the last lamp, that I have drawn close to. Are you itching to know what dear Cinnamus travelled all the way north to Liguria for? I will tell you, it was to buy a small estate in Britain near Noviomagvs, from Marcus Ostorius Scapula. Ostorius was given the estate when campaigning with Vespasian. He was with a detachment of our Atrebate allies, negotiating a peace treaty on the shore of Vectis Ins,[185] when they were treacherously attacked by the natives. Heavily outnumbered, he held them off, forming a shield-wall around the boats with the

---

[185]Vectis Ins: The Isle of Wight

few soldiers at his command; allowing the delegation and the Royal Prince, who was a Roman citizen, to launch the boats, and gain the safety of Titus' invading force waiting off shore. The fastest ships were sent to his rescue, Scapular was fighting for his life; retreating backwards into the sea, his wounds bleeding into the surf; he was the last man standing. Titus, who saw all, awarded him the Oak Leaf and the royal prince gave him the estate. Now Cinnamus has given it to me. It is not a large estate and not very profitable, it lays on the Northern edge of the chalk, with its Villa close to the London road that runs through the Estate.[186] Cinnamus thinks that it would be a suitable site for a vineyard. One day I may return with a vine culturist, but I don't fancy staying there; it is too primitive and no proper baths. Time for sleep, it has been a lovely day.

The funeral of Cinnamus has now passed. His death was a release from the torment of the Illness that struck him to the floor six months ago, that is what we keep telling ourselves to alleviate the blackness of the trauma. When it struck, the illness half killed him, one side of his body became useless and he lost the ability to speak. A long time before that, he had suffered from tiredness and pains in the head that had caused him to be irritable. After the first attack he slowly regained a few words of speech. When we were alone sitting in our rooms, he managed with great effort to summon the residue of his concentration, I moved close to him, he mumbled these words,

"Verriculla my dear" he feebly clutched my hand to his cheek with his good hand, "my death is a new

---

[186]This is now called Stane Street or the A29 You can visit the remains of a Roman villa at Bignor The location fits the text

beginning for you. You already have money, soon you shall have more. Always keep your hand on your purse string- take lovers - but beware husbands - safeguard the children- I know you are prudent. Don't be sad, tell all our friends to be happy - I shall either be once more in company of the Master, or in sweet harmless oblivion - Your life here has been dear to me - my last love and the best - the most beautiful wife, mother - and clever........."
Only a few words, words that exhausted him; words so precious, more precious than his former erudite self. He had further attacks towards the end and seemed unable to recognise people, not only the staff that looked after him, but those who knew him. It particularly distressed Paullina who had known him the longest.

We made sure he had a good blaze, and we are having a commemorative inscription erected.

CINNAMUS ANNAEUS FREEDMAN OF SENECA BORN IN TARSUS GREEK HUSBAND TO VERRICULLA WHO LOVINGLY SET THIS UP

Acte was unable to attend the funeral. She sent us a most charming letter and Paullina and I hope to see her soon, when she comes we will hold her tight, to share our grief; the Emperor is to return to Rome. When Paullina and I were relaxing in the baths together she told me rather hesitatingly,

"Before I came into the household, Cinnamus once had a lover." A little surprised that she felt the need to tell me, I cut in.

"I am sure he did, he was a very satisfying lover sometimes rough sometimes gentle, with masterly expertise in.." Paullina cut in on me a little vexed,

"Yes I know how good a lover he was; but," she bit her lip, "it was Acte who was his lover. I would not have told you but I must, for the children."

I thought of Acte standing behind us, gently comforting us, when the master was dying; Acte loves us all I thought. I hope the darling had as good a time with Cinnamus as I did, what fun it will be to compare notes and it will take her mind off her harrowing life at court. Over these thoughts the voice of Paullina was telling me not to be too distressed and how sorry she was for me to be told this.

I paid more attention to her,

"You have to know and Cinnamus wouldn't tell you, as he would not have you upset, Acte agreed that I should tell you after the funeral for the sake of Julius and Fortunata"

"How does it affect them?" I naively asked, she bit her lip again and looked down at the floor.

"They both have the same father, Cinnamus. Nero thinks the child is his, he could not be told otherwise. He thinks the child is safe and will grow up to be a great artist. When Nero made Acte his Mistress, they had to sever their love. That does not mean that Cinnamus loved you any the less. You have to know in case the two children want to marry when they grow up. I have no living children of my own and I think of you two, Acte and Verriculla as my daughters I don't want to make you jealous,"

I reassured her,

"Both Acte and I could not have a better mother, and our children a better grandmother. It is strange how we were all born at different ends of the earth and Fortuna has joined us all together as a family close to the hub of the world."

Paullina had a few tears as we held each other close.

"And how do you know of Cinnamus' prowess as a lover" I chided.

"Oh! You noticed that little slip" Her face displayed a hue of red that was not due to any increase in temperature in the baths.

"Go on" I said "we can have no secrets now, reveal all. What did you two get up to?"

She could see that I was not upset but amused by the former antics of my husband and this is what she told me.

"After we were first married, Seneca, despite his best efforts, failed to make me pregnant. We were both upset not only for ourselves, but it is considered unpatriotic not to have children. Seneca was convinced that it was his fault. When I pointed out to him that his previous wife had died in childbirth, he said that after two years of trying, they had resorted to making special arrangements. I agreed to the same arrangements. I had a wonderful time, the two men making love to me, one after the other the three of us together. Cinnamus believed that to conceive, a women has to be totally aroused and he was an expert. And we carried on in that way until my body was swollen with child. That's how I knew when I tucked you up in your wedding bed you were in for a good time, and what the outcome would be."

"Yes" I agreed, "I was just a little virgin then and he treated me so tenderly,"

It was Paullina's turn to chide me.

"A little virgin that had been giving him the benefit of her big blue eyes since the day she arrived, I should say; the poor man never stood a chance."

"For how long did the three of you carry on like that?" I don't know why I asked but I am glad I did, the answer seemed to round the subject off.

"Until I was four months pregnant, Cinnamus asked permission to carry on loving us, only as master and mistress. He was always very correct. He told no one, a lovely man, completely trustworthy."

The young attendant came to us offering a massage.

"Madam Paullina would, I am sure" I stood up and helped Paullina over to the slab, laid her down and wiped the tear from her dear old cheek with the words,

"Lucky girls we three aren't we? Enjoy the massage."
I dressed and went out.

The scribes have to be kept on their toes. Since Cinnamus died I have had to sell one scribe and dismiss another, both trouble makers. They just refused to accept the authority of their new mistress. There have been too many mistakes, too much talking, neatness of script was in decline and necessary punishments have been administered.

Appendix
How the Letters Were Discovered

November of 1992, Zagreb Pleso Airport; here I first met Geza Vermes, Doctor of Medicine, a lean middle-aged man with a welcoming smile and sad eyes. We shook hands and he led me firmly by the arm from the arrivals, lounge to his awaiting car, an old battered Yugo. Plenty of these cars had been sold in Reading, there they were considered cheap down-market cars, not the sort a doctor would be seen driving. On disembarking from the aircraft I had entered a different world from my flat in a leafy suburb of Reading. The clean modernity of Heathrow Airport London ablaze with signs and adverts contrasted to the military coarseness of Pleso, I felt the guard's cool suspicious eyes follow me as I passed through customs control, their Kalashnikovs held at the ready. It was not busy but the customs officer spoke quickly in his native Croat, I deliberately asked him to use Russian. He faltered, and disdainfully waved me through to my awaiting host.

The wind-swept environs of airports are never attractive places; the ubiquitous blocks of flats that adorn the periphery of Eastern European townscapes were evident in their towering ugliness. However, there were also the older suburbs, the pre-war houses that had been left untouched by paint or repair since the 1930's, their woodwork now bleached white, they remain unsullied by modern innovation, still resplendent in their Jugendstil and Art Deco Architecture: the communists preferring to build flats for all, rather than maintain the middle class villas. The roads had also received little attention since the 1930's, judging by the pot holes, causing Geza to snake the car from one side of the street to the other as he drove us to his home, fortunately there was little traffic. There were also no modern shop fronts, no bright lights, and thank heaven no hideous fast food chains, the streets were as empty as the shops, what a pleasant relief from Reading.

Geza's house turned out to be a moderate sized villa. I was ushered through an elegant, if a little rusty wrought-iron gate that had, I noticed, a steam locomotive motif incorporated into the design of the top rail and large stack of fire wood piled up beyond. I said, as I passed through,

"I see you are well prepared for the winter."

"It is the result of being a doctor, my country patients or their families often show their appreciation by small gifts, eggs, bacon, fire-wood and if they have been hunting, the odd venison joint, especially on the production of a healthy baby boy. It's just as well on my salary, if I get it, otherwise we would all starve. Come on in, there will be a good fire and a bottle of schnapps to welcome us."

It was true; he led me into a well proportioned room with a blazing log fire and an old suite of red leather upholstered arm-chairs that proved remarkably comfortable. He filled two small glasses with schnapps, we clinked glasses together and downed the colourless spirit in one swallow, then simultaneously gasping for breath as the alcohol rasped our gullets. Wiping his eyes and looking at me with a good measure of embarrassment he said in a hoarse whisper,

"Excuse me, I don't usually drink, but thought it impolite not to greet a guest without the traditional salutation."

After recovering composure and adopting a more upright stance, I replied while wiping my eyes,

"That was fiery, I don't drink either, and I thought you would consider me impolite if I refused".

My confession caused joint chuckles and that was the beginning of our friendship.

Geza excused himself from the room and returned leading by the hand a young lady. She had a coy charming smile and sensitive eyes. He introduced his wife Angela. We shook hands and I felt her sensitivity quite penetrating. They have no children. We sat by the fire chatting, while Angela organised dinner. Their cook had superbly prepared a hare served with carrots and potatoes, followed by honeyed walnuts; truly fresh food, much superior to the supermarket produce I daily eat. I wondered what medical procedure Geza had performed to procure such tasty fare.

Over the next two days, Geza related the story of the finding of the letters. It transpired that his grandfather had held the position of manager at the railway works in Zagreb prior to the Second World War. Geza apologised for the family history lesson he was about to relate; I put him at his ease, and he started.

"To learn the business from the bottom up, my grandfather put his eldest son Lica, my uncle, to work on the factory floor. There he met and came under the influence of Josip Broz, who was organising the metal workers into a union. Josip Broz had joined the revolutionary Red Army in 1917. There he learnt the art of guerrilla warfare and how to organise and lead men. Broz was arrested as a communist agitator outside the railway factory gates and imprisoned under the 1921 Protection and Public Security Order. An order introduced after an unsuccessful assassination attempt on the king and a successful shooting of the communist's main political rival. My grandfather might well have had a hand in Broz's arrest. Broz at the time was in his opinion, 'a dangerous trouble maker' in the railway works and a bad influence on his eldest son. During 1937, the now released Broz fought in the communist ranks in the Spanish civil war. Using his underground network that he had created throughout Yugoslavia, he recruited solders to Spain. Again, my grandfather used his influence, he guessed my uncle wanted to join Broz but prevented him from getting a passport. Passports in 1937 were only issued for visiting the Paris exposition. Eleven thousand were issued; few went to Paris, many went to Spain. Broz survived the fall of Spain to the Fascists, escaping through Paris to Slovenia. Here using a new alias, Tito was ready after the 6th April 1941 Axis invasion of the Balkans, to rally a partisan army."

Angela brought in a tray with a pot of hot coffee, a jug of cream, buttered scones and a jar of wild berry jam. She plied us with the coffee and spread a liberal covering of the jam onto the scones. Geza continued after we had eaten, Angela sat on the floor resting against his legs and looking into the fire.

"A great deal of political animosity had grown between my grandfather and my uncle in the past. Not that grandfather supported Ante Pavelic's Ustashas. They were a pro–fascist party and had succeeded where the Communists failed: shooting the King and collaborating with the invaders, they were to be responsible for many atrocities. However, this time grandfather allowed my twenty one year old uncle to join the partisans forming in Slovenia, with his blessing. Grandfather, now ever more abhorring the strident cruelty of the omnipotent Nazi regime that controlled the railway and the fifth columnists Ustashas who were massacring the Serbs; he considered Tito (Broz) the best option.

At this time, my father joined the works in Grandfather's office, where grandfather kept a close eye on him. My father quickly learnt German. His job was assisting with military train movements, although the Italians controlled Croatia, through the N.D.H. (Ustashas), Germans controlled the trains. I don't know how, but he discovered he had a flair for languages, useful when dealing with the Nazi officials and Fascist Italians." Geza broke off and went into the hallway, he pulled out from the cupboard under the stairs a British Army 303 ammunition box, the wooden type with rope handles. He put it on the floor by his arm chair, sat down, opened the lid and pulled out a worn and battered brown note book. From it, he took a scrap of paper, browned and iron marked by time.

"This is all I have of uncle Lica. It has the name 'Bohinjska' north east path, tree line, east 2k, written on it." He carefully passed it to me, I held it gingerly on the flat of my hand, I noticed the ink had faded too. He held the book open for me, and I slipped it back between the pages.

"Where is Bohinjska?" I asked, he ignored my question and re-opened the book at a marked page. As he did so, he continued the history lesson.

"My father's wartime diary, this is the entry for June 14th 1941." He smiled and read from the book. "Met brother L at the old signal box. He told me that he had joined Tito's staff and that I should ingratiate myself with the Germans. Useful information I was to pass on by leaving notes in certain secret places. I must gather Information on troop-trains and particularly movements of arms, as the partisans would need them for the coming struggle. L. told me the first task he was given was to find a suitable place to set up a long range radio receiver-transmitter, to contact Russia. L. had set out into the mountains with a guide, a local shepherd. Disguised as hunters, with the radio in a rucksack, the shepherd led him to a cave with a stunted tree growing over the mouth, its roots hanging down like an unruly moustache. L. tied a large stone to a length of cord and threw it over a high branch of a tree standing a short distance from the cave. Then affixed the aerial wire to the cord and hauled it up over the branch, securing it to a lower branch. He then pulled it tight from the other end and secured it to the tree over the cave, allowing it to hang down he twisted it around the hanging roots and pushed it into the cave. The inside was not spacious but adequate, just enough head-room if you stood in the middle and just enough light for the radio operator. That is all he had to do, the radio operators would stay there and they would bring the accumulator. However, after he unpacked the radio he connected the aerial and pushed the copper earthing rod into the cave floor, it went in a few inches and stopped, he picked up a fallen stone and hammered the rod. It had hit something, but not hard like stone, He pulled out the rod and examined the pointed tip, it gleamed silver. Quickly, he scooped away the dusty earth to reveal a metal box covered in a light-grey powder except, where the point of rod had scratched and dented the metal; there it was shiny bright. He covered over the box, repositioned the rod and wired it up to the radio set, to lessen the risk of a later discovery. He did not tell the shepherd who was puffing on his pipe outside. He wrote down the instructions of how to find it, and told me to keep it safe, and to trust no-one! We should not meet again until after the war and that if he did not survive I was to investigate the cave.

My father took a considerable risk in recording his meeting with uncle Lica. Fortunately, he remained safe and undetected by the U.C.L collaborators otherwise there would be no one to tell the tale." Geza shut the book, although I think he related these incidents from memory.

Geza's grandfather shortly after the war received a letter from Marshal Tito. Informing him, 'Regrettably Captain Lica Vermes died in action in Serbia in 1945. He has requested that his brother be given a scholarship as a reward for the useful intelligence he had provided during the great patriotic war.'

Influence at the top is always useful, and father took full advantage. He studied the theory of ancient Languages, Greek and Latin, at the Russian State Humanities university's Institute of Linguistics, fortunately he started before the schism with Stalin ; grandfather kept his old job and this old house.

It was not until 1952, after father had completed his studies at Moscow and settled into a teaching position at Belgrade University, that he set out to unearth uncle Lica's war-time discoveries. To answer your question, Bohinjska Bistrica is about 130k west of Zagreb in the Julijske Alps."

"That is in Slovenia" I interrupted,

"Yes, that is where the cave is, in the mountains above the town. Father journeyed there by train, decked out for a walking holiday, with boots and rucksack and booked into a pension."

Geza reopened his father's book and started to read,

"There are two paths into the mountains, they both pass through a ridge of lower hills that guard the way to the high peaks. I follow instructions and take the higher one behind the church, it is steep going and I soon reach the top. Before me is a pastoral valley with the wooded mountain side opposite. There are the tracings of a path leading across the valley ascending into the wood; my only option is to follow it. I cross the valley and struggle up this path for some time. It was better defined than it first looked; perhaps shepherds use it to bring their sheep to the high summer pasture. Unaccustomed exertion and altitude is causing nausea. I rest awhile before my lungs explode: I need a cigarette.

Eureka! I have found it! When I emerged on to the high pasture, there were paths running East and West along the tree line, probably made by sheep or goats. I paced out the 2k east, kept my eyes open wide and there it was, betrayed by the aerial wire still hanging in the trees. I have thrown off my rucksack and unpacked the small garden trowel I thought to bring with me; my writing is shaky; is it exertion, or excitement? If it is possible to be disappointed and elated at the same time, that is my present state. I have found the lead box: I have not brought a tool to open it; I wonder at my stupidity. It is too heavy to carry and I fear that it might contain something breakable, or why would the contents be so well protected? Coin-hoards for instance are often deposited in bags or pots, not lead boxes. I resist the urge to pummel it open. I have re-buried the box and thought of Lica doing the same eleven years ago. I wish he was here now. I will return; equipped.

Today, I have travelled to Ljubljana. In the market, the only thing on offer suitable for cutting through lead was an old surgical saw. For this, I have bartered away my last cigarettes. Tomorrow will reveal all!

I have made the same journey as two days ago, except on this occasion I have walked past the cave in my excitement, and seemed to spend an interminable and exasperating time back and forth looking for it.

The lead box is exposed. Will the saw open it? Yes, I carefully cut away at a corner parallel to the top. I angle the saw and make short strokes so as not to damage the contents. My impatience is not rewarded; I have foolishly tried to tear the top off unsuccessfully. I rest, craving for a cigarette before continuing with the saw. I am amazed, stupid why didn't I guess! Codices, bound in wood, three volumes! I can hardly believe it. Ancient writing on velum, remarkable condition. Thank God I was careful with the saw. Carefully, I have wrapped my treasure in the old clothing carried with me for that purpose and put them into my rucksack. I shall now hastily return home."

Geza closed the book and removed from the ammunition box three hard backed A4 sized writing books. He opened the first book and handed it to me. Affixed to the inside cover was a pre-war black and white photograph.

"My father, uncle and grandfather, taken on holiday by grandmother" he told me. The inscription read 'Venice summer 1936.' Apart from the Gondolier in the striped shirt, Grandfather was wearing a dapper pin-striped suit, with a gold watch chain displayed across the front of his well filled waist-coat. A twisted waxed moustache adorned the proud face, his head topped off with a bowler hat; one hand held a large cigar the other a silver capped cane. He looked every inch a prosperous middle class gentleman. Uncle Lica, a youth of about sixteen, was wearing a light suit with baggy trousers, two-toned brogues and a straw boater, he was leaning on the shoulder of his young brother, a boy of about nine: the future father of my host.

The page opposite was inscribed,

'In memory of Papa and my brother Lica, who are united in death after being reunited in sprit and affection through a war that tore many families apart' To whom I have dedicated these translations within these folios. Geza Vermes, professor of Classics, Belgrade.

In addition, added in Geza's hand writing. 'To grand-Mama, who died after a long illness 1989, Aged 95.'

"Is Madame Vermes, your mother, still alive?" I asked,

"Yes, she still lives in Belgrade, prefers to live there amongst her old friends and papa's old colleagues. I asked her to move back here when Grand-mama died, but she refused,"

"Did your grandmother suffer much before she died?" I queried.

"Just the typical problems of the geriatric, it was a sad time, I have lived in this house with her since I graduated and started my practice at Zagreb Hospital. Luckily for me Angela came to nurse her, and I never let her go."

He looked adoringly at Angela, who stood up, leaned over the back of his chair and stroked his head. She spoke in a soft voice with her eyes lowered.

"George has had a long day," referring to me.

"Now, it is time for bed, tomorrow when refreshed he will much better be able to study all"

She bent over and kissed him on the forehead and with the words,

"Come, come", she offered her hand to assist him out of the armchair.

She was more forceful than I at first expected. Next, it was my turn; to refuse that charming hand; it was impossible.

Geza returned the books that I was impatient to study to the ammunition box. Escorting me to my room, he explained, that Angela is always right. She was right: I had a job to stay awake to write up my notes!

I slept later than I intended and arose to find that Geza had been called out on an emergency. Angela sat me at the breakfast table and ordered boiled eggs, a selection of cold meats, bread, butter and honey. The cook called to her when it was ready and Angela fetched it in, explaining that the cook, who was her aunt, preferred to stay in the kitchen. I think that as an ex-communist Angela felt a little guilty about staff.

"It is necessary to have help" she explained, as she was often working at the hospital or accompanying Geza on his medical expeditions. She poured the coffee. I noticed she abstained and when I refused the top-up, she poured some for herself. I concluded that coffee was in short supply; I could have brought some tea bags.

"What does Geza want to do with his father's manuscripts?" I asked her.

"He wants to publish them in the west; we need the money to buy medicine and equipment, our hospitals were in a poor condition before perestroika and now we have civil war to make it worse. Why is it always the innocent that suffer? We in the Balkans have suffered one oppressive regime after the other, one faction set on another for hundreds of years. President Tito under the slogan 'Brotherhood and Unity' maintained a peaceful Yugoslavia until his death in 1980. After the split with Stalin in '48 we gained help from the west, we set up factories and became quite affluent. After perestroika Yugoslavia fractured back into the old states and they fractured into antagonistic communities. Now there are Greek-Orthodox Christians, Catholic Christians, Muslims and Communists; all led by thug politicians who rose to the surface by preaching hate in their communities; and leading their moronic armies in horrific attacks on their neighbours, murdering boys and raping girls; although we are all the same people, speaking dialects of the same language, the same race! Except for the Muslims from

Afghanistan who, with their Al-Qaeda organisation, support the Bosnia and Croat Moslems, they come from all over the Arab world. The world does nothing while the degenerates think it glorious fun to maim, rape and kill their unfortunate neighbours, they call it ethnic cleansing; all in the name of greed and power!"

Her Russian was not as fluent as Geza's and she was angry, she wiped away a tear and repeated in a softer voice,

"You should see the state of our hospitals here in Croatia now. A spreading conflict is the last thing we need. We long hoped for a better world, but it just seems to get worse. We hoped you could advise and help by publishing Geza's Papa's translation and with the sale of uncle Lica's original find. We need the money to buy drugs and equipment, all our money is spent on arms, or is swallowed into corrupt pockets. Geza's uncle died in 1945 not fighting the Germans, but, fighting the Albanians who had been armed by the retreating Germans, and were attacking Serbia. 40,000 troops descended on Albania. Before that when the partisans and the Chetniks weren't fighting the Nazis, they fought each other"

Saddened by the state of affairs, I said lamely,

"I had better get started; shall I sit at the table by the window?"

We carried the ammunition box over to the table, she one end and I the other. Angela opened it for me and on leaving the room told me to call out if I wanted anything, as she would be in the kitchen listening out. As she left I wanted to go with her and comfort her, telling her that things always get better. I then thought of Northern Ireland, and the NATO bombs recently destroying the hapless conscripts of the Iraqi Army and parts of Baghdad. I picked up the first book of the Russian translation.

After a glance at the photograph, I turned to the first double page of Professor Verme's translation. He had translated the letters into Latin on the left page and Russian on the right. At the head of each letter, he had assigned a letter of the Greek Alphabet and to the left a generous margin for notes.

All hand written in ink, quite legible, with plenty of notes in the margin. My Latin is not on a par with Professor Vermes, so I mostly worked with the Russian.

Geza returned home in the early evening, he looked tired and a little dejected. He had been called out to a local farm; a small girl had cut her finger on a bread knife the day before. Fever from blood poisoning had set in. Despite taking her to the hospital, with all the relatives that could fit into the Yugo to supply blood, she died. He said,

"Of course, it would have been better if they had taken her to the hospital immediately. Transport is always a problem and farmers are independent people. Although the hospital has run out of anti-biotic vaccine, we could have cleaned and sutured the wound. A strong dose of penicillin when I first arrived might have saved her; if I had one, who knows?" He sighed with shrug of the shoulders, "Have you read the letters?"

"I have, they are very interesting, particularly as they mostly concern the Western Roman Empire.

"Will they sell in the West?"

"Translated into English they would have a moderate sale and I guess they would make a little money, but as the readership is limited to those who have an interest in Ancient History, you are unlikely to make a fortune."

"What about selling the originals?" he asked looking a little sadder.

"It's not a market I know. However, I would guess, they would fetch a considerable sum!"

His face looked a little brighter. I felt rotten about disappointing him again, particularly after he had had a hard day.

"First though you must prove ownership. They were found in Bohinjska, Slovenia; taken to Belgrade, Serbia, where they were kept by your father, and now they are in your hands in Zagreb, Croatia. All of these states and towns may lay claim to them. Second, you must prove that they are genuine. Provenance is all important. I must warn you that some people will say that your father manufactured the whole thing. To counter them and satisfy the market, the original letters will have to be studied by experts and subjected to date testing. Therefore, you will have to employ international lawyers and experts, all very expensive and time consuming!"

He smiled with downcast eyes.

"Yes, I expected as much, nothing in life is ever simple. They ought to belong to the people of Slovenia: the land that harboured them for so long."

"I suppose it is obvious that your uncle did not want them to fall into the hands of the Germans; but why did your father keep them secret all his life? He must have been itching to tell his colleagues. He would have been famous and the name of his brother would have gained renown!"

"That is so but Stalin and the Communist States at that time were eager to show that slavery was a tool of Capitalism and that slaves were a repressed and downtrodden class. As you allude to in your book 'Slavery in the Roman World' that this is not always the case, as is made evidently clear by these letters. Consequently, he feared that his own career would suffer and the safety of the letters might be in jeopardy if their existence were known. As an insurance against the contents of the letters being lost to posterity, he recorded and translated them into the books you have been studying and then kept them separate: giving them to me to keep. The original letters are now here with me. I collected them from my mother for you to look at. I feel it is safer to have them here, should anything happen to her."

"I certainly would enjoy the privilege of looking at them, But, I can't give you an opinion on them, as I don't know enough about ancient codices" I sat looking around expectantly.

After a pause, Geza said,

"I am surprised you haven't looked at them already."

I frowned; he nodded towards the ammunition box.

"They're in there under the false bottom! Papa made it, pull the little tag." After removing the contents, I pulled the little tag and the false bottom lifted off. The inside had been lined with felt, there, in three depressions as in a jewel case, wrapped in brown paper, were the codices. A pair of white cotton gloves lay on top, I put them on. Using both hands I lifted one out using the ribbon that had been placed underneath to facilitate this and unwrapped it.

"Papa believed these copies date from the ninth century, he did not think they are a forgery from that date, or they would not have taken the trouble to include all that insignificant detail about Britain. Just looking at it, it does not look anything special, just strange writing on parchment. Papa thought it the most important find in modern times! If you are familiar with the Greek or Roman script, the Croatian Glagolitic alphabet of these codices resembles neither, although some letters are based on cursive Greek others are thought to be Slavic-runes compiled by the ninth century saints Cyril and Methodous." Surprised, I thought it was based on Greek.

"This should be in the hands of a conservator," I thought, as I reverently re-wrapped and placed them safely back in their box!

"I think you should inform the appropriate government departments of what you have in your possession. At the same time photograph samples of the codices, date them and send copies to all the major world libraries with an account of how they came into your possession. Ask your mother to sign a statement, that your father bequeathed the codices and his translations to you. You must also ask your lawyer to establish world copyright. Although I don't know whether it is possible to copyright old writings, you should be all right in copyrighting the translations. On second thoughts make the copyright your priority."

The following day, we three drove a little way into the country and walked through woods of evergreen oaks. We discussed the best plan, concluding that first we should seek legal assistance. I advised that in the west, legal advice is easily available when however the lawyers smell big money, they take big fees; watch out!

I volunteered freely to render Professor Vermes' Russian Translation into an English version that I hoped would be popular. To be published at the time of maximum publicity, after the ancient letters had been revealed to the world. He agreed that the post war paper of which Professor Vermes' writing books consisted, was not of the best quality, being covered in iron marks and rather frail. Copies should be made quickly and sent to me to work from as soon as possible. Big white snow flakes gently descended on us as we walked back to the car. I noticed, sitting behind her, how they melted into Angela's thick black hair as she carefully drove us home around the holes in the road. We parted on the following day with hugs and good wishes. I could see them in the clear morning air, two diminishing figures in winter coats, he standing close with his arm around her, both waving at the Boeing 727 as it circled to gain height. If Angela's bleak expectations were correct, how could these precious letters be entrusted in the hands of a state, reminiscent of Nazi Germany with its concentration camps and mass graves? As I looked down, between the wispy clouds, the peaks of the rugged blue-white, snow-crested Alps shone in the high sun. I wondered what previous catastrophe had caused the codices, so precious, to be hidden there.

When the package arrived from Geza with the copies of his father's translation, the accompanying letter told me that for the time being he would hold the codices until more benign times. He and Angela were going to work in the war zones; he expected to be busy. He thanked me for my help and told me to take my time with the work: there is little hope of an improvement in the near future.

Letter received May 1993,

Slobodan Milosevic's Serb Army continue their ethnic cleansing policy; we do what we can. My greatest fear has happened: Angela is missing, her guards were shot, and she abducted. We are in a nightmare of rape and murder; if her flesh survives I know what will happen to her mind. Grief, hope and despair. Pardon my tears dampening the paper. I only have a moment to write and cry. The U.N. observers are still observing from a distance.

Geza Vermes

Why should it be Angela! Beautiful Angela, with her long black hair, her soft kind face and shy brown eyes; why should she be rent from her lover into the abyss of violence, away from the warmth of their affection. Why do men make victims of the innocent? We may shudder at the cruelty and victimisation contemporary with the time of the letters; but today the pustules of inhumanity break out on the skin of mankind wherever they are not suppressed and they are slow to heal and often hidden.